Rein

Cruise Ship  Series

Book 3

Hope Callaghan

Visit my website for new releases and special offers: hopecallaghan.com

Acknowledgments

Thank you to these wonderful ladies who help make my books shine - Peggy H., Cindi G., Jean P., Wanda D., Barbara W. and Renate P. for taking the time to preview *Reindeer & Robberies,* for the extra sets of eyes and for catching all of my mistakes.

A special THANKS to my reader review teams, here in the U.S., and those across the pond, over the border and an ocean away.

Alice, Amary, Barbara, Becky, Brinda, Cassie, Charlene, Christina, Debbie, Dee, Denota, Devan, Diana, Diann, Grace, Jan, Jo-Ann, Joyce, Jean K., Jean M., Katherine, Lynne, Megan, Melda, Kat, Linda, Lynne, Pat, Patsy, Paula, Rebecca, Rita, Tamara, Valerie, Vicki and Virginia.

CONTENTS

iv

Cast of Characters

Mildred Sanders. Mildred "Millie" Sanders, heartbroken after her husband left her for one of his clients, decides to take a position as assistant cruise director aboard the mega cruise ship, Siren of the Seas. From day one, she discovers she has a knack for solving mysteries, which is a good thing since some sort of crime is always being committed on the high seas.

Annette Delacroix. Director of Food and Beverage on board Siren of the Seas, Annette has a secret past and is the perfect accomplice in Millie's investigations. Annette is the "Jill of all Trades" and isn't afraid to roll up her sleeves and help out her friend in need.

Catherine "Cat" Wellington. Cat is the most cautious of the group of friends and prefers to help Millie from the sidelines. But when push comes to shove, Cat can be counted on to risk life and limb in the pursuit of justice.

Danielle Kneldon. Millie's former cabin mate. Headstrong and gung ho, Danielle loves a good adventure and loves physical challenges, including scaling the side of the ship, scouring the jungles of Central America and working undercover to solve a mystery.

And there were in the same country shepherds abiding in the field, keeping watch over their flock by night. And, lo, the angel of the Lord came upon them, and the glory of the Lord shone round about them: and they were sore afraid.

And the angel said unto them, Fear not: for, behold, I bring you good tidings of great joy, which shall be to all people. For unto you is born this day in the city of David a Saviour, which is Christ the Lord.

And this shall be a sign unto you; Ye shall find the babe wrapped in swaddling clothes, lying in a manger.

And suddenly there was with the angel a multitude of the heavenly host praising God, and saying,

Glory to God in the highest, and on earth peace, good will toward men." **Luke 2:8-14 King James Version (KJV)**

Chapter 1

"Out with the old. In with the new." Millie dropped the glittery jack-o'-lantern in the bin and dusted off her hands. "It's a good thing Sharky found some extra storage space for Andy's fall festival goodies."

"Wait. I've got one more." Danielle tossed a spray of burnt orange leaves on top. "Ever since he won the fall contest, he's going crazy with the decorating."

Andy Walker, the Siren of the Seas cruise director, recently won a contest against rival cruise director, Claudia, from the Baroness of the Seas.

Because of his "big win," he'd skipped over decorating the ship for Thanksgiving and only added a few cornucopias and some artificial corn displays to go along with the pumpkins and his now infamous smelly scarecrows.

Guests were beginning to question the Halloween decorations, and Millie insisted it was time to take them down. Finally, Andy agreed.

Unfortunately, for Millie and Danielle, their boss decided to put them in charge of packing everything up, which was what they were doing while the ship was docked in St. Martin for the day.

"What's on your schedule tonight?" Danielle asked.

"I'm hosting an early round of *Killer Karaoke*, followed by introducing the headliner comedy show and then it's off to the *Heart and Homes* passenger contest. How about you?"

Danielle rolled her eyes. "*Mix and Mingles*. I wish Andy would find someone else to host it. Isla would be a much better fit."

"He must think you do a good job. Better you than me." Millie's radio began to squawk. It was Andy.

"Go ahead, Andy."

"Where are you?"

"Danielle and I finished packing up the Halloween decorations, and now we're heading out to make our rounds."

"Perfect," Andy's voice boomed over the radio. "Meet me on the stage. I have a big surprise."

"10-4." Millie slipped her two-way radio back on her belt. "I wonder what's up."

"Andy and surprises are two words that don't belong in the same sentence," Danielle quipped.

"No kidding. Let's get this over with." Millie and Danielle took a shortcut through the crew only area. They looped around before making their way to the other end of the ship.

Millie slowed, waiting for her friend to fall into step. "How's it going with your new cabin mate?"

"Carlah is great. She leaves the cabin early in the morning and is gone all day."

"She works in the specialty coffee shop?"

"Yes." Danielle nodded. "And you'll never guess who hangs out there all of the time now."

"Cat?"

"Nope. Amit. I mentioned the other day to Carlah how Amit seemed to have taken a sudden interest in the specialty coffees. Her face turned red, so I think there might be a little love in the air," Danielle singsonged.

"I may have had a hand in introducing the two in a roundabout way." Millie opened the theater door. "I sent Amit up there on a fact-finding mission a couple of months ago."

"Millie the matchmaker," Danielle teased.

"Now I need to find you a steady beau."

"Thanks, but no thanks."

The stage curtains swayed, and Millie caught a glimpse of movement off to the side. "What is that?"

"I have no idea."

"Something tells me it involves Andy's big surprise." Millie pulled the door shut behind them, giving it a quick tug before taking a tentative step.

She caught a whiff of cinnamon, peppermint and something else.

"It smells like Christmas," Danielle whispered. "Maybe Andy is finally ready to work on the Christmas holiday theme. Has he mentioned it to you?"

"No. I figured he would start adding seasonal activities any day now. He has to. Thanksgiving is already over."

The back section of the theater was dark. Millie waited for her eyes to adjust before warily making her way down the center aisle. As she drew closer, she could hear Andy humming as he moved back and forth across the stage.

"He's humming *Deck the Halls*," Danielle said. "I think you're onto something with the Christmas theme."

Millie came to an abrupt halt near the front of the stage. "What in the world?"

Andy hustled to join them. "Well? What do you think?"

Chapter 2

Millie stared at the array of reindeer. There were large wooden reindeer, stuffed reindeer and cardboard cutout reindeer. There were even small tea light holders, shaped like miniature reindeer. "Reindeer."

"Yep," Andy beamed. "Now that you finally took down all of the Halloween decorations, I figured it was the perfect time to decorate for Christmas."

"We...we decided to take them down," Danielle sputtered. "Millie has been nagging you for weeks to pack up the Halloween stuff. What's up with the critters?"

"It's a new contest." Andy explained he'd purchased the array of reindeer after reviewing his yearly budget and discovered some leftover cash in his slush fund.

Millie eyed the reindeer suspiciously. "What kind of contest?"

"We're going to put these reindeer all over the ship, some hidden and some in plain sight. Starting with our next group of passengers who are boarding on Saturday, we're going to pass out these reindeer tracking sheets. I had them designed especially for the contest."

Andy handed Danielle and Millie a sheet of paper.

"Tracking sheets?" Millie studied the long slip of paper, mentally counting the number of empty lines. "You're hiding twenty-five reindeer?"

"Not quite. Flip it over. There are more on the back." Andy made a flipping motion.

Millie flipped the paper over. "You mean to tell us you're going to hide fifty reindeer all over this ship?"

"Close." Andy had the good graces to look slightly embarrassed. "You and Danielle are going to hide the reindeer."

"You're kidding," Danielle gasped.

"You're crazy," Millie corrected. "Is that why you called us down here...so we could take these..." She trailed off as she motioned toward the array of reindeer.

"Yes. I'm putting you and Danielle in charge of hiding them." Andy cleared his throat and reached into his front pocket. "I assembled a list of suggested hiding spots. I think we should pick a few easy ones so our junior passengers can play along and then some more difficult spots for the passengers with a sharp eye."

Andy handed each of them a sheet of crumpled paper as he rambled on with his suggestions. "Keep in mind the reindeer need to be hidden in public places...the restaurants, the lounges, the library and the gift shops."

Danielle lifted a hand to cut him off. "Some of these reindeer look heavy. You can't expect Millie and me to lug these all over the ship not to mention *hide* them."

"I've enlisted the help of Reef in maintenance to transport the bulkier reindeer. He's on his way here now." Andy caressed one of the reindeer's wooden antlers. "You should've seen me trying to get these babies on board the ship."

"It couldn't have been nearly as difficult as it's going to be trying to hide them," Millie muttered under her breath.

"I'm sure you two will find some clever hiding spots. Now don't forget to keep a list of exactly where you hid all fifty so that come January when you have to gather them all up you don't forget any."

"There he is now." Andy motioned over Millie's head.

A scowling Reef Savage, Sharky's counterpart and the ship's nighttime maintenance supervisor, trudged down the center aisle. "You better make this quick. I ain't got all day."

"It won't be quick," Danielle warned. "We have fifty reindeer to hide."

"I suggest you let Reef help place the larger reindeer and then you and Millie can work on hiding the rest. Since the contest doesn't start until the next set of passengers board, you have plenty of time."

Andy clapped his hands. "Reef can't hang around here all day chit-chatting. If each of you grabs one of the larger reindeer, you can knock three right off the list."

The women huddled with Reef as they discussed the placement of the larger reindeer. Millie wisely suggested the shorter the distance to lug the larger creatures, the better off they would be.

The trio each grabbed a bulky critter, placing the first one, a stuffed reindeer complete with a jingle bell collar, in the stage's sound booth.

The reindeer, Danielle dubbed "Dancer," peered over the Plexiglas where he would be partially visible to the younger passengers as well as the adults.

A second reindeer, this one wooden, found a home next to the theater's bar area and a third slightly smaller one, behind the marquee sign and the display case.

"He's cute." Danielle stepped back to admire the ceramic reindeer sporting a red cardigan and matching scarf.

"Three down and forty-seven more to go," Millie said.

Reef consulted his watch. "I've got fifteen minutes tops before I have to head downstairs for an emergency maintenance meeting."

Millie perked up. "An emergency meeting?"

"It's technically a meeting for both the maintenance department and housekeeping. The higher ups started combining our meetings to save downtime," Reef explained. "I haven't heard the official reason, but Sharky said one of the passengers on deck ten was robbed last night."

"Robbed?"

"Yeah. I don't have the details. Patterson is gonna tell us what happened. I'm down to ten minutes if you want me to finish helping you," Reef said.

"Yes, of course."

The trio returned to the stage, and each of them grabbed another of the larger reindeer. They placed one in a chair behind the excursions desk. The second, a ceramic reindeer, found a home in the spa's hot tub area, draped in a towel, poised to take a dip.

Millie decided the last of the large reindeer would join the diners in the main dining room, at the server station.

She dug around inside the cabinet and pulled out a chef's hat, which she promptly perched atop his head. "He looks hungry." She moved a basket of fake fruit in front of him.

"I gotta get going."

The women thanked Reef before he took off, leaving Millie and Danielle alone in the dining room.

"Let's grab a kitchen cart and load a bunch of the smaller reindeer on it," Danielle suggested. "It will save us from having to make a ton of trips back to the theater to get more."

"That's a great idea, but first I want to find out about the theft," Millie said. "I'm surprised Andy didn't mention it."

"He was too wrapped up in his reindeer. I'm sure it slipped his mind."

They headed down the stairs to deck zero and the maintenance area. Millie and Danielle made it as far as the bottom step before other ship crewmembers blocked their path and where Dave Patterson, the head of security, began to speak.

"I would like to start by thanking everyone for taking time out of your busy schedules for this emergency meeting. This morning, one of our passengers on deck ten reported a theft."

Dave Patterson went on to explain he was in the process of investigating the matter, but wanted to remind all of the housekeeping staff and maintenance crew it was essential that guests' cabin doors remain closed and locked at all times, even during daily cleaning.

"We take ship crimes seriously. Our guests need to know both they and their belongings are safe on board the Siren of the Seas."

One of the ship's crewmembers raised his hand. Patterson pointed to him. "Yes?"

"Can you give us a little more detail on what was taken, so we can keep an eye out?"

"That's an excellent question." Patterson winced. "Unfortunately, the passenger claims cash was stolen from their cabin safe."

"Cash," Danielle whispered in Millie's ear. "Out of their safe?"

Millie had never heard of a complaint of theft from a passenger's safe. "I wonder which cabin steward covers that area."

"I don't know, but I'm glad it's not me," Danielle said.

Kimel Pang, the head of housekeeping, traded places with Patterson. He repeated Patterson's statement. He asked them to remain vigilant and on the lookout for suspicious behavior, and ended with a stern reminder that any employee caught stealing would not only be fired, but also prosecuted to the fullest extent of the law.

The meeting concluded. Millie waited until the stairwell cleared before making her way to Patterson, who stood talking to Sharky and Kimel.

Patterson lifted a brow as Millie approached. "I would like to say I'm surprised you're here, Millie. Then again, maybe I'm not."

"Reef told us about the meeting while helping Danielle and me with a decorating dilemma. He said he was heading down here for an urgent meeting regarding a theft. Andy never mentioned it."

"That's because Andy isn't involved in security and neither are you," Patterson said pointedly. "This matter involves housekeeping and security."

"Yes, but wouldn't it make sense if all of the staff, especially those of us who are with the guests full time, were on alert as well?"

"Don't make a mountain out of a molehill. My guess is this is an isolated incident," Patterson said.

Millie ignored the comment. "Is it possible the passenger is lying?"

"Of course. My team is investigating all angles." He changed the subject. "I see you removed the Halloween decorations."

"Yes, Andy finally let us take them down. We're moving onto the reindeer invasion, which reminds me...Danielle and I still have about forty more reindeer to hide around the ship."

Patterson chuckled. "Another Andy contest?"

"What else?" Millie shook her head. "Ever since he won the bet against Claudia, he's gone cuckoo over contests."

Danielle, who was chatting with another of the housekeeping staff, wandered over. "We better get back to work before Andy hunts us down and hounds us about the reindeer."

"Good luck with your investigation." Millie told Patterson good-bye, and they exited the area. "Let's head to the galley to borrow a kitchen cart from Annette."

The breakfast rush had ended, and since it was a port day, the galley wasn't busy.

Millie bounced on her tiptoes and glanced inside the porthole. She could see Amit standing at one of the counters and caught a glimpse of Annette passing by. "The coast is clear."

The women slipped inside and stood off to the side watching Annette, the ship's director of food and beverage, bark orders to her kitchen crew as the workers darted back and forth.

Millie silently slipped in behind Amit and peered over his shoulder. "Whatcha' making?"

Amit stumbled back, clutching his chest. "Miss Millie. You got me again."

"Sorry," Millie apologized. "I didn't mean to scare you. What are you working on now?"

"The Caribbean Christmas barbecue up on the lido deck." Amit grabbed a juicy barbecue rib with his tongs. "You must taste. Miss Annette is testing a new barbecue sauce."

Danielle eased in next to Millie to inspect the contents of the bowl. "What about me?"

"Of course, Danielle." Amit placed a small slab of ribs on a plate and slid it toward Millie. He eased a second set on another plate and handed it to Danielle.

"The official taste-testers have arrived." Annette hustled across the room to join them.

"My timing is impeccable." Millie pinched the ends of the tender rib and took a tentative bite. A droplet of sauce dribbled down her chin.

"This is delicious." Millie closed her eyes and savored the tangy barbecue mingled with a hint of sweet. It was the perfect combination for the melt-in-your-mouth meat treat. "I've tasted some delicious barbecue, and this is hands down one of the best."

"I agree." Danielle tore off a large piece of meat and popped it into her mouth. "I could easily devour an entire plate of these ribs."

"Sorry. I can only spare a few samples. You can come back later to see if we have any leftovers," Annette said. "I'm sure you didn't drop by just to sample my food."

"No, but these are definitely an added bonus." Millie polished off the rest of her ribs and reached for a napkin. "We're here to see if we can borrow an empty kitchen cart. We have some reindeer to hide."

"Another Andy project?" Annette guessed.

"Yes, who else?" Danielle reached for another rib.

Annette's hand shot out, and she playfully swatted Danielle. "No more goodies."

"We came from Patterson's crewmember meeting. One of the guests' cabins up on deck ten was broken into last night," Millie said.

"Bad news travels fast," Annette said. "It's a big mess, and that's not all."

Chapter 3

"Do not tell them, Miss Annette." Amit waved frantically. "Gusti will be upset."

"It's okay. Millie and Danielle are our friends." She turned to Millie. "Gusti, the room steward, accidentally left the guest's cabin door ajar."

"That's terrible. Patterson and the security team think the cabin door wasn't shut properly and someone snuck in?"

"If it even happened," Danielle said. "I mean, what are the chances a passenger's cabin door is accidentally left ajar, someone sneaks in and steals an undisclosed sum of cash?"

"It does sound suspicious," Annette agreed.

"Gusti, he say the passenger bragged about winning big in the casino," Amit said.

"So maybe he lost money in the casino and is reporting a theft to cover up his loss." Millie glanced at her watch. "We better get back to work finding those reindeer a new home before Andy starts blowing up my radio."

Millie and Danielle thanked Annette and Amit for the tasty barbecue samples and then rolled an empty cart out of the galley. They wheeled it down to the theater and began loading the reindeer.

All of them fit, with the exception of a couple of the smaller ones. Danielle shoved those in her jacket pocket.

After loading the reindeer, they consulted Andy's notes and suggestions on hiding them before working their way from deck three all the way up to deck fifteen and the VIP area.

The task took longer than Millie anticipated, leaving her barely enough time to grab a sandwich at the deli before making her way downstairs for a round of *Killer Karaoke*.

The passengers trickled in, and the requests began piling up. During a short break between songs, Millie consulted the growing list. "I'm sorry folks. I'm going to have to cut off the requests."

She was almost through the list of singers and requested songs when her radio went off. It was Andy.

"Hey, Millie. Where are you?"

Millie stepped off to the side and pressed the talk button. "I'm hosting *Killer Karaoke* in the atrium. I have about three more songs, and then I'm moving on to my next event. What's up?"

"Our new comedian hasn't boarded the ship yet. His taxi is stuck in traffic. I need you to host a round of trivia to entertain the guests until he arrives."

"A round of trivia? That will go over like a lead balloon," Millie predicted.

"I have no choice. Besides, it will only be one round. Offer the players a special prize to placate them."

"You mean a ship on a stick isn't a dandy prize?" Millie teased.

"Of course it is. Maybe you could throw in a spa discount or gift shop discount card."

The karaoke singer was nearing the end of his song. He shot Millie a terrified look. "I gotta go. I'll squeeze in one more song here and then head to the comedy venue. Have I told you lately you owe me?"

"Yes. All of the time. Thanks, Millie."

Millie turned her radio down and sprinted across the stage to rescue the singer. "I have some bad news. I only have time for one more song before I have to leave." She consulted her clipboard. "Jean and Jen, you're up."

A mother/daughter duo took the stage for a rousing rendition of *Santa Baby*, one of Millie's least favorite Christmas tunes.

While they sang, Millie began placing the karaoke supplies inside the cabinet. There was a sharp jab on her left shoulder, and she glanced up to find a passenger glaring down at her.

"I want to sing my song, *A Star is Born*."

"I'm sorry." Millie offered the woman an apologetic smile. "Something has come up. I have to leave early."

"But it's my turn." The woman clenched her jaw and continued glaring at Millie.

"I have no choice, but to end the karaoke early." She closed the cabinet and attempted to slip by the woman. The angry passenger darted to the left, blocking Millie's path.

"If you don't let me sing, I'll lodge a complaint at guest services."

Millie heaved a heavy sigh. "I hope you don't do that." She had a sudden thought. "Tell you what...the next round of karaoke starts at seven-thirty. I'll put your name at the top of the list, and you can be the first on stage."

A man quietly stepped in behind the woman. "C'mon, Tracy. I think this is a fair compromise. Let her put your name at the top of the list and we'll come back."

"I don't want to come back." The woman stomped her foot in frustration and Millie resisted the urge to point out it wasn't a matter of life or death.

Instead, she glanced at her watch. "I am sorry. I have to go. I'll keep your name on the list in case you change your mind." She brushed past the woman and hurried out of the room.

Millie made a quick stop at the trivia cabinet near the casino where she grabbed some pads of paper and a handful of pencils before racing down the stairs to the comedy venue.

Her heart plummeted at the sight of the packed room. The woman's disappointment was nothing compared to Millie having to face a room full of guests who were expecting a comedian.

Millie grabbed the stage mike and briefly explained the comedian was stuck in traffic and she would be hosting a round of trivia while they waited for his arrival.

Although there were a few grumbles, most of the guests stayed for her Caribbean-themed trivia game.

The game ended and there was still no sign of the comedian. "I'm going to take a quick break to see if there's an update." Millie hurried out of the room and into the corridor. "Andy, do you copy."

"Go ahead, Millie."

"I need an ETA on the comedian. I finished the round of trivia. The natives are getting restless."

"Joe Gaffin, the comedian, just boarded and should be arriving any second."

"Awesome." Millie reluctantly began making her way back inside the comedy club when she spied a man strolling down the corridor at a fast clip.

Millie hurried to greet him. "Joe?"

"No." The man shook his head, confused. "Dave."

"Sorry. I thought you were someone else."

Another man, this one shorter and with dark curly hair, sprinted toward her.

"Joe Gaffin?"

"Yes, ma'am. You must be Millie. Sorry that I'm late."

"No need to apologize. I'm glad you're here." Millie escorted him into the comedy club. "I'll head back to the stage to give you a quick intro."

She grabbed the microphone and returned to the stage. "I'm sorry to disappoint you folks, but I won't be hosting another round of trivia. Instead, I would like to introduce the Siren of the Seas' comedian, Mr. Joe Gaffin."

The man stepped onto the stage.

"Good luck." Millie thrust the microphone into his hand and exited stage left.

It was time for her to start preparing for the *Heart and Homes* show, one of the more popular passenger participation events.

Millie mentally ticked off her to-do list, including choosing the participants and reviewing the questions.

Thankfully, Felix, another of the ship's entertainment staff, was already there. The two narrowed down the contestants to three couples - a newlywed couple, a decades-old married couple, and Millie was certain they'd hit the jackpot when a couple celebrating fifty years volunteered to participate.

By the time Felix and she finished explaining how the game worked, the theater was full.

Millie had only hosted the show on a handful of occasions. Felix was an old pro, so she accompanied the women off stage while he asked the spouses a series of questions.

Felix radioed Millie after he finished, and the women returned to the stage, swapping places with their spouses.

Millie kept the conversation light, asking the men if they were enjoying their cruise, if they enjoyed St. Martin and about their plans for the rest of the week before they joined Felix and the spouses back on stage.

"Thank you, Millie," Felix said. "We'll start with the ladies and Marie on the end. If your husband was stuck in traffic, which one of your relatives would he least like to be in the car with?"

"My relative?" Marie shifted in her chair, looking slightly uncomfortable.

"Yes." Felix nodded. "If your husband was sitting in his car stuck in traffic, who on your side of the family would he least like to be in the car with?"

"Well...I would have to say my cousin, Eric."

"Your cousin, Eric," Felix repeated. "Why your cousin Eric?"

Marie shot her husband a glance. "Because he has an annoying habit," she blurted out.

"What kind of annoying habit?" Felix smiled, waiting for Marie to elaborate.

"He smells everything."

The audience began chuckling.

"It's pretty gross. He smells everything around him...clothes, furniture. He even smells other people's shoes."

Felix made a gagging noise. "Maybe he's sensitive to odors."

Marie nodded emphatically, and Felix moved on to the next contestant.

The answers were entertaining, and when Felix finished asking all of the questions, Millie tallied up the results.

He passed the mike to Millie for her turn to question the men. She made it through the first round when there was a sudden commotion coming from the audience, near the front of the stage.

"I can't hear you!"

Millie peered into the crowd, struggling to see beyond the bright stage lights. "I'm sorry. I'll turn up my volume." She fumbled with the buttons on her microphone. "Is that better?"

"No!"

Frustrated, Millie turned the volume up again. The speakers screeched loudly and the audience groaned.

"Sorry." She quickly turned it back down.

Felix rushed to Millie's side and adjusted the microphone. "Try that."

"Is that better?"

"Yes," someone called out.

"No!"

Millie squinted her eyes in an attempt to pinpoint the audience member who was complaining. Her heart skipped a beat when she realized it was Tracy, the same woman she'd encountered during *Killer Karaoke*. Their eyes met, and the woman grinned evilly.

"I do apologize." Millie turned her attention to the contestants, but all the while, she could hear the woman, Tracy, complaining loudly.

The game show finally ended, and Felix announced the winners, the newlywed couple.

Millie thanked everyone for joining them and ended with a reminder the next round of karaoke would be starting soon.

The theater started to empty. Millie could still hear Tracy's loud grumbling.

Determined to clear the air, Millie handed the mike to Felix. "I'll be right back." She marched across the stage and down the steps.

"I'm sorry you didn't enjoy our *Heart and Homes* show. As I pointed out earlier, ending the karaoke show before you had a chance to sing was beyond my control." Millie reminded the woman her name was still at the top of the list if she wished to participate in the second round.

The woman smirked. "Will you be hosting the karaoke?"

"Yes." Millie nodded. "Would you like to be the first to sing?"

"No. I have no intention of singing, but I'll be there. You can count on it." The woman's threat hung in the air as she sprang from her seat and sauntered out of the theater.

The man who was with her, the same one she'd met at the karaoke earlier, reluctantly stood. "I'm sorry..." He glanced at Millie's nametag. "Millie. Once my wife gets something in her head, she has a hard time letting it go."

"What do you mean, 'she has a hard time letting it go?'" Although Millie asked the question, she had a sinking feeling she already knew the answer.

"She's holding a grudge, at least for now."

Exasperated, Millie threw her hands in the air. "Why doesn't she just sing her song?"

"I wish she would." The man smiled apologetically and then trudged up the center aisle, trailing behind his wife.

Millie stomped up the steps and joined Felix on stage.

"What is her problem?" He nodded toward the exit.

"I ended the *Killer Karaoke* session early. The woman, Tracy, was next up to sing. When she found out it wasn't going to happen, she wasn't very happy."

"So she started heckling you?" Felix's eyes widened.

37

"I guess so. From what her husband said, she's holding some sort of grudge against me."

"It was a song for heaven's sake."

"I even offered to let her be the first to sing during the next karaoke session."

"Did she take you up on it?"

"She said she would be there, but had no intention of singing." Millie's shoulders slumped.

"She's a crazy stalker," Felix said.

"I hope not. It's going to be a long night."

"No." Felix shook his head. "We're not playing that game, Millie. You and I are gonna swap places. I'll host your *Killer Karaoke* if you want to take my bingo."

Millie pressed a hand to her chest. "Seriously? I would be forever indebted. Maybe by tomorrow, she'll forget all about me."

"Let's hope so." They finished clearing the area, and Millie shooed Felix away to start the karaoke while she began setting the stage for the evening round of bingo.

Another of the ship's staff joined her. Much to Millie's relief, Tracy never showed. The bingo ended, and Millie began making her rounds starting at the top of the ship, working her way down as she swung by the events to make sure everything was running smoothly.

She passed Danielle on the lido deck, and they chatted briefly before Millie kept moving. Her final stop was the piano bar.

Her feet were beginning to ache from standing all day. Despite a slight limp, she decided to stop by the atrium to check on Felix.

She waited near the back until she caught his eye. He motioned her off to the side. "You're never gonna guess what happened."

Chapter 4

"Tracy, the woman who was harassing me, never showed up," Millie guessed.

"Oh no." Felix shook his head. "She was here, sitting right in the front row. She hung around for a couple of songs, and then I think she realized you weren't going to be here, so she left."

"Unbelievable." Millie shook her head. "Who does that?"

"Crazy people." Felix twirled his finger near his temple. "They are everywhere."

"Thank you for rescuing me."

"No worries. We got to take care of each other, you know?" Felix winked at Millie and then headed back to the stage to continue the karaoke.

The long day finally caught up with Millie, and her steps dragged as she climbed the stairs to the bridge. She slipped her keycard in the slot and quietly pushed the door open.

Evenings on the bridge were her favorite time of the day. It was peaceful, almost serene, the exact opposite of Millie's busy days hosting activities.

The dimmed lights gave off a warm glow, accompanied by the low hum of the navigational equipment.

Staff Captain Antonio Vitale was on the bridge, standing next to Millie's husband, Nic.

"Hello, Millie."

"Hey, Antonio, Nic."

"How was your day?" Nic asked.

"Crazy busy. Andy is working on a new contest. He put Danielle and me in charge of hiding reindeer all over the ship." A yawn escaped Millie's lips. "Excuse me."

"You look tired." Nic placed a light hand on her shoulder, and Millie studied her husband's face. "You look tired, too. I think it's time to call it a day."

Nic promised to join his wife shortly, and Millie finished the short walk to their apartment.

Scout, their teacup Yorkie, met her at the door. He pounced on Millie's shoe before circling her legs, demanding she pick him up.

Scout pawed at her chin, her nametag and then lunged forward to nibble on one of her earrings.

"I wish I had half your energy." She carried him onto the balcony and set him on the deck. The move sent a sharp pain down Millie's back.

"Ouch." She reached behind her and began massaging the sore spot, which is where Nic found her moments later.

"Maybe we should sign up for a couple's massage."

"It sounds heavenly," Millie said. "I'm not sure why, but today was tough, even though it was a port day."

"Tomorrow is a sea day with an even busier schedule." Nic slipped an arm around his wife and kissed her forehead.

"Don't remind me," Millie groaned.

Scout trotted over, and Nic picked him up. "Maybe you should bring Scout along with you tomorrow. He spent some time with me on the bridge today and kept watching the bridge door. I think he was waiting for you."

"He was?" Millie's heart melted as she gazed at her pup's face. "I'm sure he's bored. I'll bring him along for my sunrise stride tomorrow morning."

"But for now..." Nic motioned them indoors. "I'm ready for bed."

Scout took his usual place smack dab in the center of the bed. Millie was careful to give him plenty of room. After Nic and she finished their prayers, she rolled onto her side and promptly fell asleep.

Millie woke early the next morning, realizing she forgot to grab the day's schedule. She quickly dressed, and she and Scout headed downstairs, beating Nic out of the apartment.

Danielle was already in Andy's office discussing the schedule.

He watched Millie and Scout make their way inside. "Danielle told me you finished hiding the reindeer."

"We did, and I even remembered to make a list."

"Perfect." Andy nodded approvingly. "Send me a copy."

"I'll have Scout remind me." Millie set him on the conference table, and he pranced to the other side to greet Andy.

Andy scratched the pup's head. "I was thinking of ordering a mini reindeer costume for Scout."

"You'll be wasting your money. Remember the hot dog costume you bought him for Halloween that he refused to wear?"

Scout greeted Danielle and then trotted across the table waiting for Millie to pick him up. "I'm here because I forgot my schedule."

Andy untacked a sheet from the bulletin board and handed it to Millie.

"Thanks." She scanned the schedule and shoved it into her pocket. "I better head out. Scout and I are hosting the sunrise stride this morning."

"I ran into Felix last night on my way home," Danielle said. "He said something about a passenger harassing you yesterday."

Millie sucked in a breath. "Don't remind me."

"Harassing you?" Andy looked alarmed.

"It's a female passenger, the one who was upset when I ended the *Killer Karaoke* early yesterday." Millie briefly explained how the woman followed

45

her around. "After she started harassing me at the *Heart and Homes* show, Felix insisted on swapping events. He hosted karaoke, and I hosted his bingo."

"This is a serious matter, Millie. Please let me know if she continues to harass you."

Millie lifted her hand in mock salute. "Will do." She lifted Scout's paw and waved good-bye. "Here's to all of us having a fabulous day."

Danielle followed Millie out of the office. "The woman sounds like a crackpot. Andy is right. You better be careful."

"What's she going to do...throw me overboard?" Millie joked.

"That's not funny. People do crazy stuff and you need to be on your guard."

"I will," Millie promised.

The women parted ways near the stairs, with Scout and Millie heading up to the jogging track. Several passengers were already there waiting.

"What a cute pup." One of the women patted Scout's head. He let out a small yip and licked the woman's hand.

"Thank you for joining Scout and me for the sunrise stride." Millie explained one lap equaled a quarter mile and they would complete four laps for a full mile.

The skies were beginning to brighten, but the sun hadn't come up yet, keeping the air a bit cooler. Millie set the pace, and her mood lightened as she thought about the day's events.

At the top of the list was the VIP pampering party in the spa. It was Andy's latest brainstorm, and a way to reward the platinum and diamond guests with complimentary light facials and manicures.

Millie was impressed with Andy's generosity until he finally admitted he'd heard from one of the other ship's cruise directors, that by offering the VIP pampering party, the spa sales increased over a hundredfold.

The feedback from the newly offered event was positive, and Andy was right, the spa product sales and paid services soared. It was a win-win for everyone.

Next up, Millie was hosting a game of bridge in the library followed by an ornament decorating class.

The Christmas ornament project was new to Millie, and although she wasn't particularly creative, she was willing to learn.

After finishing the fourth and final lap, Millie thanked the participants for joining her. One of the passengers, a young woman, lingered behind to say good-bye to Scout.

"I almost didn't come this morning."

"I'm glad you did," Millie said.

"Me, too." The woman scratched Scout's chin. "My sister and I were worried something would happen."

Millie tilted her head. "Whatever did you think would happen?"

"It's kind of early, and there aren't too many people up yet. It would be the perfect opportunity for someone to rob me."

Millie pressed her palms together. "Our ship has topnotch security. You're safe on board the Siren of the Seas."

The young woman wrinkled her nose but remained silent.

"Did something happen?" Millie prompted.

"Yes. The cabin next door to us was burglarized last night while the couple was at one of the nightclubs."

Chapter 5

"I...did they report it to security?"

"Yes." The woman nodded. "That's how I found out. The head of security visited our cabin early this morning to ask us if we'd heard or seen anything suspicious last night."

"Did you?"

"Sort of. My sister and I stopped by the piano bar for a singalong, and then we stopped by the pizza place to grab a snack. When we got back to our cabin, we noticed the neighbor's door was ajar. At the time, we didn't think too much about it."

A cold chill ran down Millie's spine as she remembered the comment about the first passenger who claimed someone stole money from his cabin and his door was found ajar.

Although there were surveillance cameras all over the common areas of the cruise ship, there weren't any cameras in the cabin hallways, only near the elevators and stairs.

The young woman glanced around and then lowered her voice. "I feel terrible...like maybe we should've checked it out."

"There's no reason to blame yourself. Besides, if someone was inside the cabin next door robbing it, the last thing you should do is put yourself in a dangerous situation." Millie didn't mention the other theft to the already frightened young woman. "Just be sure to keep your cabin door shut and locked. I'm sorry...I don't think I caught your name."

"Amy. I'm here with my sister, Carley. This is our first cruise. My parents would freak out if they knew what happened."

Millie did her best to reassure Amy she was safe on board the Siren of the Seas, but even she was beginning to wonder after two passenger thefts in as many days.

She remembered Patterson's meeting with the maintenance crew and housekeeping staff. He had reminded all of them to keep an eye on the rooms, to ensure the passenger doors were shut and locked when they finished cleaning.

Amy interrupted Millie's thoughts. "I also feel bad because the security guy asked us about our room steward, Gusti, and if we remembered seeing him or his cleaning cart in the hallway when we turned in last night."

"Your cabin steward is Gusti?"

"Yep." Amy's head bobbed up and down. "Our cabin is on deck ten."

A wave of nausea washed over Millie. Gusti was also the room steward for the other theft victim.

Surely, Gusti was not the culprit. He would be the first person security questioned.

"I better head back to the cabin to change. Carley is insisting on taking a spin class this morning." Amy thanked Millie for hosting the sunrise stride before giving Scout another pat on the head and walking off.

After Amy left, Millie mulled over the recent thefts. She wondered how often passengers reported missing items from their cabins and how often the room stewards were blamed.

Crimes of any nature were grounds for immediate dismissal and reported to the local authorities for prosecution. Surely, Gusti wouldn't jeopardize his job or risk being arrested for a few quick bucks.

"I better take you back home." Millie dropped Scout off at the apartment before making her way to the *Waves Buffet*.

It was still early, and the buffet area was relatively quiet. Passengers typically slept in on sea days, after a late night or a busy port day the previous day.

She eased a breakfast burrito onto her plate and added a scoop of hash brown rounds along with two slices of limp wheat toast.

Millie stopped to grab a cup of coffee and then made her way to the corner, to a window seat with an unobstructed ocean view. Off in the distance, she caught a glimpse of another cruise ship, heading in the same direction.

The holiday season would end soon. Spring was right around the corner, and the Siren of the Seas would be embarking on a new adventure, heading across the ocean to their temporary home port of Southampton, England.

Since finding out about the repositioning and new itinerary, Millie was researching the stops in Ireland, Scotland and France, not to mention the UK.

Her list was lengthy, and she realized the upcoming summer season would fly by before the ship returned to Miami and the Caribbean ports for the winter season.

"Hey, stranger." Danielle waved a hand in front of Millie's face. "I called your name. You must not have heard me."

Millie watched Danielle place her plate of food on the table. "I was thinking of the British Isles and all of the things I've been researching."

"I can hardly wait." Danielle unwrapped her silverware. "I backpacked through Europe during my younger, wilder years, but I haven't been back since."

"I thought *these* were your younger and wilder years," Millie teased.

"This is tame compared to my past." Danielle changed the subject. "So what's on your agenda today?"

"I'm in charge of the VIP pampering party in the spa. I'm also hosting a bridge game in the library followed by decorating Christmas ornaments, all before tea time at three o'clock. How about you?"

Danielle rattled off her schedule. "Andy radioed me a few minutes ago...something about a brief all-employee meeting. It starts in about twenty minutes. He didn't call you?"

"No." Millie fiddled with the dial of her radio. "Crud. My radio was off. I bet he tried."

"We have enough time to eat and then head down to his office. I wonder what new crisis occurred."

"Maybe he's getting another shipment of reindeer he wants us to hide."

Danielle rolled her eyes. "Don't give him any ideas."

The women gobbled their breakfasts and dropped their dirty plates in the bin near the door before heading down the steps.

Andy was just starting the meeting when the women arrived.

He droned on about ensuring a fun-filled sea day and rolling out his new Christmas theme before moving on to safety. "We've had two unfortunate and preventable thefts of passenger possessions during the last couple of days. Although you're not in passenger cabin areas, at least I hope you're not, you are with the passengers most of your working hours. Please be on the lookout for any suspicious activity."

Andy answered several questions before dismissing the group.

Millie waited for the crowd to clear and began following them out.

"Millie." Andy motioned her back inside the room. "I have a special project for you."

"Another one?" Millie grumbled. "Promise me it doesn't involve reindeer."

"As a matter of fact, you and Danielle did such a bang up job of hiding the reindeer; I came up with a brilliant idea for the Christmas theme this year...reindeer."

"Reindeer? I mean, it's not like I have anything against reindeer, especially Rudolph. What about Jolly Old Saint Nick and the cute Christmas elves?"

"I have plans for them, too. Don't worry. I'm calling it the Siren of the Seas' reindeer games."

"That's catchy. It reminds me of Rudolph."

"It is catchy. The passengers will love it." Andy settled into his chair. "Have a seat."

Millie reluctantly sat. "I'm warning you I'm not going to wear reindeer antlers, a red nose or a hot, furry costume. Reindeer games remind me of the song where the other reindeer picked on Rudolph."

Andy ignored the comment as he slid a holly green sheet of paper toward Millie. "This is one of the games I'm rolling out. Instead of the standard trivia, we're - meaning *you're* - going to host a Christmas riddle matchup.

"A riddle matchup?" Millie slipped her reading glasses on. "What do elves learn in school? The elf-abet."

She read another one. "Name a group of people afraid of Santa Claus."

"I know the answer," Andy said. "Claus-trophobics."

"What did Santa change his name to after sliding down the chimney where the fire was still burning?"

"Crisp Kringle." Andy crossed his arms. "Isn't this more fun than the same old run-of-the-mill trivia games?"

"Good grief." Millie scratched her chin. "These are corny."

Andy's face fell, and Millie could see she'd hurt her boss' feelings.

"They're corny but cute." Millie waved the sheet of paper. "I think I can make this work."

"I'm glad you're on board with the reindeer games," Andy brightened. "I also have plans to add a Christmas-themed scavenger hunt. I ordered a batch of Christmas bingo cards. They should be waiting for us when we dock in Miami Saturday morning."

"What about Christmas food dishes?"

The last time Andy offered suggestions, he and Annette had gone 'round and 'round. He might be able to get away with assigning special tasks to Millie because he was her boss, but Annette? No way.

"I do have a list of ideas I want to share." Andy fumbled inside his pocket and pulled out a folded sheet of paper. He handed it to Millie. "She's not keen on me butting in on her territory, so I thought you could drop this off for me."

"I'll drop it off. Whether it will do any good is another story."

"You're the best, Millie."

Millie glanced at the sheet. "I guess I better get going. I'll swing by the galley on my way to the VIP pampering party."

Andy followed Millie to the door. "I knew I could count on you, Millie. I'm working on lining up visits from the jolly old elf himself down in the atrium. I figure we could add a couple of North Pole elves and some special gifts for the youngsters."

Millie stepped out of Andy's office. "Why haven't you included Danielle in these fun-filled festivities?"

"I have. She doesn't know it yet." Andy smiled slyly. "We got such positive feedback when she supervised the teen scene for Halloween, I thought I would let her run the teen Christmas activities, too."

Andy continued. "The official start of our reindeer games is on Saturday when the next group of passengers board. Feel free to make some copies of the Christmas riddle matchup and swap it out at your next round of trivia for a trial run."

"Will do." Millie gave her boss a thumbs up and then made a beeline for the galley.

She started to ease the door open when a loud beeping caught her attention. Alarmed, she stuck her head around the corner where a thick cloud of smoke filled the air.

Chapter 6

Millie's eyes and nostrils stung as she struggled to see through the thick layer of smoke.

The galley's smoke alarms blared loudly. Through the haze, she spied Annette, fire extinguisher in hand and peering into one of the ovens.

"Stop the racket before Sharky shows up with a firehose." Annette waved to Amit, who anxiously hovered beside her. "The smoke is starting to clear."

She set the extinguisher on the counter, yanked her chef's hat off and began fanning the oven. "Amit, go get some floor fans. We've got to get this smell cleared out pronto."

Amit shot Millie a look of panic as he raced past her and out of the galley.

Much to Millie's relief, the fire alarms grew silent. The only sound left was the low murmur of voices as the kitchen workers waited for Annette to speak.

"The show is over. It's time to get back to work. We still have thousands of hungry passengers to feed."

Millie crept toward her friend, who stood with her back to her, her shoulders hunched. "I would ask how your morning is going. Maybe I don't want to know."

"It was going pretty good until one of my new kitchen workers walked away from the stove, failing to notice my brunch bake was bubbling over." Annette slipped on a set of oven mitts, reached into the oven and pulled out two large pans of breakfast bake.

"They don't look any worse for the wear." Millie leaned over her shoulder to inspect the food.

"The food can be salvaged. My oven is another story."

"I didn't know you hired new kitchen help," Millie said.

"It's only temporary…at least I hope it's only temporary. I'm a sucker for sob stories," Annette shoved her hand on her hip. "I guess we could do a quick taste test to make sure the bakes are still edible."

"If nothing else, you can serve it in the crew dining room," Millie suggested. "I'll give it a try."

Annette carved out two generous squares of the breakfast bake, placing each on a separate plate. She handed a plate and a fork to Millie, who sawed off a chunk and took a small bite.

"It's hot." She took another tentative bite, savoring the salty ham and a generous amount of tangy shredded cheddar cheese. "It doesn't taste burnt at all."

Annette blew on her bake and closed her eyes as she took a big bite. "You're right. It's definitely edible."

Amit returned to the galley lugging an industrial size floor fan. He placed it in front of the stove and plugged it in.

"Turn it on low. It shouldn't take long to air this place out," Annette said.

"Yes, Miss Annette. The smoke, it is already clearing," Amit said. "Gusti feels terrible about the oven. He said he only walked away long enough to check on the bacon."

"I can't put all of the blame on Gusti. It's partly my fault. I don't have time to properly train him."

"Gusti, as in the room steward Gusti?" Millie asked.

"Yes," Amit nodded. "When Miss Annette found out Gusti was pulled from his job cleaning cabins and with nowhere else to go, she offered to let him work here."

65

"You already heard about the second theft incident," Millie guessed.

"Yeah. Poor guy can't catch a break," Annette said. "Donovan pulled Gusti from the work schedule until Patterson and his men finish investigating. When Amit told me what happened, I offered to let him help out here in the galley."

A dark-haired man with somber eyes hustled toward them. "Miss Annette, I am sorry."

"It's okay, Gusti. The bake is fine. My oven? That's another story."

"I will clean it." Gusti clasped his hands. "I like to clean."

"I'll show you where we keep the kitchen cleaners." Amit led his friend away, and Millie waited until they were out of earshot.

"I ran into a passenger whose cabin is next door to the one that was broken into last night. She said Gusti's cleaning cart was in the hall when she and her sister turned in for the night. It appears the theft occurred while the passengers were in one of the late night lounges."

"Did you hear the cabin door was ajar - like the previous theft?" Annette asked.

"Yes. Doesn't it seem suspicious? I mean, think about it. Gusti would know enough to make sure the doors were shut, especially after the first incident."

"I agree. Seems to me that whoever is stealing from the passengers on deck ten wants it to look like an inside job or is trying to throw Gusti under the bus," Annette said.

"Do you know what was taken?" Millie asked.

"Nope. Gusti doesn't know, either. Patterson and his men aren't talking. I'm sure they're downstairs tearing Gusti's cabin apart right now."

"You can't blame them. Two thefts in two days is suspect. The fact they were both on deck ten and in Gusti's area looks bad."

"I agree." Annette eyed Millie curiously. "What are you doing here this early in the morning?"

"I'm on my way to the spa for the VIP pampering party. I just left Andy. We went over his new Christmas-themed schedule."

"I'm waiting for him to show up with his 'suggested' list of holiday-themed foods any day now."

"Now that you mention it..." Millie gave her friend a sympathetic look.

"Andy sent you up here."

"Sort of. I haven't looked at his list yet." Millie pulled the sheet of paper from her pocket and handed it to Annette.

"Let's have a look." Annette cleared her throat. "At least he's more organized this time around and broke it down into categories. We have appetizers, entrees, side dishes, desserts and drinks."

She crumpled the note and tossed it into the nearby trashcan. "Right now I have more important things to worry about."

Millie grinned. "I'm sure you do. I better get going. It's a shame about the smoke. I'm sure Gusti will be more careful next time."

She waved good-bye to her friend and darted out of the galley, colliding head-on with Sharky, who was making his way inside. "Hey, Sharky. You here to check on the smoke alarms?"

"Yeah. One of the maintenance guys said he heard it going off. I thought I would run by to make sure Annette didn't set the place on fire."

"It wasn't Annette. It was one of her new kitchen workers. Some grease dripped onto the oven's heating element. She has it under control."

"I better check it out anyways." Sharky puffed up his chest and marched into the galley. "Heard you guys set the galley on fire."

Annette's voice rang out. "Don't you have better things to do than to harass the kitchen staff?"

Millie grinned. If she had more time, she would've hung around to watch the fireworks. She picked up the pace, making her way to the spa on deck twelve where she joined a small group of women who were chatting in the hallway.

Camille Bessette, the spa's manager, joined them and began collecting their invitations. "Thank you for joining us for our exclusive VIP pampering event. We'll start with a mini facial, using our own patented technology to cleanse, extract and hydrate all skin types. Our pamper products will leave your skin quenched, glowing and radiant."

One of the VIP guests interrupted. "Are you offering any specials on your products if we decide to purchase them?"

"Of course," Camille beamed, displaying an evenly aligned mouth full of pearly white teeth. "I'm offering an additional five percent off if you purchase today, at the conclusion of our pampering party."

She continued. "Today's party is extra special. In addition to the mini facial, we're offering a complimentary mini massage." Camille described the massage therapy as a way to soothe muscles and relieve stress and tension.

"Our mini massage improves posture, circulation and flexibility. It helps relieve tension-related headaches; it also strengthens the immune system."

"I could use that," Millie mumbled under her breath.

"Me, too," one of the women whispered. "I can hardly wait."

The spa manager wrapped up her presentation, and then several of the spa staff led the women down a long hall to the treatment rooms.

Soft soothing music, accompanied by the fragrant aroma of lavender, wafted in the air. An employee handed each of them a fluffy white robe, and after changing, the women gathered in the main treatment room.

Millie's therapist, the same woman she'd worked with on her previous visit, led her to a lounge chair. As the woman massaged her face, Millie wondered how she'd gotten so lucky to be a part of the spa services activity, and a tinge of guilt filled her.

Perhaps Danielle would enjoy a spa day. Millie made a mental note to offer to swap with her the following week.

After the mini facial, the massage therapist began massaging Millie's back, and she started to doze off.

"We are done." A soft voice woke Millie from her nap, and she blinked rapidly. "What happened?"

"You fell asleep. You looked so peaceful, we didn't have the heart to wake you," Camille said.

"I was out like a light." Millie glanced at the clock on the wall. "Is it really ten-thirty?" She swung her legs over the side of the table. "I'm hosting a bridge game in fifteen minutes."

Millie jogged to the changing area where she threw her clothes on. She joined the staff at the front desk and handed the massage therapist a ten-dollar tip. "Thank you for the facial and massage. It was wonderful. I feel a little guilty with all of this pampering. I'm going to ask Danielle, one of the other entertainment staff, to fill in for me next week."

The woman slipped the ten in her pocket. "Thank you, Millie."

Millie turned to Camille, who stood nearby. "Well? Did you sell some spa goodies?"

"That and more." Camille nodded enthusiastically. "Each of the ladies booked another massage. One even booked a couple's massage, and they all purchased some fabulous spa products."

"I'll be sure to let Andy know it was another successful event." Millie waved good-bye and dashed out the door, managing to arrive at the library with a couple of minutes to spare.

The bridge games took longer than Millie anticipated. By the time the last game ended, it was after noon, her stomach was grumbling, and she was beginning to feel light-headed.

She followed the last bridge player out, locking the door behind her.

Millie started to pass by the *Ocean Treasures* gift shop when she caught a glimpse of her friend, Cat, who was chatting with a guest near the window display.

Cat motioned Millie inside. "I haven't seen you around since you were in here hiding a reindeer."

"Andy is keeping us hopping. He's going all out on his new holiday theme, calling it the reindeer games."

"It sounds intriguing."

"We'll see. The jury is still out. You staying busy up here?"

"Oh yes." Cat nodded. "Have you heard about the thefts?"

"I have," Millie said. "Hopefully, Patterson will get to the bottom of what is going on and clear Gusti from suspicion, so he can get back to work."

"That won't be happening anytime soon," Cat said. "Brody was here about an hour ago. He told me Patterson placed Gusti in the ship's holding cell."

Chapter 7

Millie's mouth fell open. "Patterson arrested Gusti? Did Gusti confess? Does Patterson have evidence?"

"I don't know. All I know is Patterson interviewed several of the passengers on deck ten, and after he finished, he tracked Gusti down in the galley and escorted him out."

"That's terrible. He seems like a nice man."

"Those are the ones you gotta watch out for," Cat said.

"I better let you get back to work." Millie passed the galley, her thoughts on poor Gusti. Maybe he was responsible for the thefts, although it didn't make any sense. Of course, he would be the prime suspect. Maybe he wanted to be caught...or maybe he didn't do it. Either way, Gusti was having a very bad day.

Millie's quick bite to eat consisted of a mound of mushy rice mixed in with an equally mushy vegetable she guessed was broccoli. A sprinkle of almonds gave it a light crunch, but the teriyaki sauce was too sweet for her to finish eating it.

She dumped the uneaten food in the recycle bin and made her way to the *Marseille Lounge*, the location of the ornament-decorating event.

Several passengers followed her inside and she began placing a tray of delicate glass ornaments at each table.

Next, Millie added an array of acrylic paints and egg cartons filled with colored beads to the tables. Because space was limited as were the supplies, guests were required to sign up ahead of time. All fifteen spots were filled.

Millie reached for an apron to protect her work uniform and froze when a familiar voice grated loudly in her ear. She squeezed her eyes shut before sucking in a breath and slowly turning. She came face-to-face with Tracy.

"Hello." Millie forced a smile, her tone light. "Welcome to our ornament-decorating event."

"Yes." A slow smile spread across the woman's face. "Hopefully, you won't screw this up like you did yesterday during the karaoke and the *Heart and Homes* show last night."

Millie ignored the snide remark and motioned to a seat. "Please find a place to sit." Thankfully, several more participants wandered in, and she hurried across the room to greet them.

She waited for the rest of the participants to make their way inside. "Thank you for joining me for our first ornament decorating project of the season." Millie explained the guests would have a full hour to personalize their ornaments. She pointed to the array of decorating supplies and then told them she would be available to help.

As soon as Millie finished her brief explanation, Tracy snatched one of the delicate ornaments from the tray and promptly dropped it on the floor where it shattered into a million tiny pieces.

"Will you look at that?" Tracy grunted. "What kind of cheap junk are you trying to peddle?"

Millie stared at the fragments in disbelief. She began to count backward, resisting the urge to jerk the woman out of her chair and escort her out of the lounge.

Instead, she did the next best thing and made a dash for the exit. Millie stepped into the hall and snatched her radio from her belt. "Danielle, do you copy."

She began to pace and pray. "Please, Danielle. Please answer."

"Go ahead, Millie."

"Where are you?"

"Getting ready to host the behind the scenes tour. Why?"

"I need your help. I need to swap events."

"Now?"

"Yes. Right now. My stalker is back, and she's breaking ornaments in the *Marseille Lounge*."

"What?"

"I don't have time to explain. Can we swap?"

"Of course. I'm on my way."

"Awesome. I owe you one. Where are you meeting your tour group?"

"On the Riviera deck, in front of the *High Seas Art Gallery*."

"I'll head there now." Millie cast a quick glance inside the lounge and hurried down the hall where she ran into Danielle near the elevators. "The group is probably wondering what happened to me."

"Don't worry. I've got it covered." Danielle paused. "What does the troublemaker look like?"

"Her name is Tracy. She's tall and thin with straight black hair. She has small beady eyes and a sharp pointed nose."

"You make her sound like a witch," Danielle joked.

"I'm beginning to wonder."

Millie thanked Danielle again and raced to the art gallery, where a small group of guests waited. "There's been a change of plans. I'll be filling in for Danielle."

Her first job was to ensure the passengers were properly attired or more specifically, no one was wearing flip-flops.

"I see you all got the memo on wearing close-toed shoes. Before we begin our tour, we'll watch a brief video presentation." Millie led them inside the empty room and made her way to the small stage.

She'd watched the video during her orientation, but missed the part where Majestic Cruise Lines was one of the first cruise lines to sail out of the Port of Miami, and in fact, helped build the port.

The presentation ended, and Millie waited by the door for the group to join her. "We're going to start our tour in my favorite part of the ship, the theater."

While they walked, Millie shared her story, how she started with the Siren of the Seas as the assistant cruise director.

"I heard you're the captain's wife," a woman said.

"Yes. Captain Armati and I married this summer." She didn't elaborate, and the comment always made Millie slightly uncomfortable. It wasn't that she cared if they knew but secretly wondered if the passengers might treat her differently if they discovered she was the captain's wife.

She thought of her stalker, Tracy, and wondered if somehow she knew Millie was married to the captain. Could that be the reason the woman was harassing her? Anything was possible.

They stopped briefly backstage where Millie rattled off the list of shows. She led them through the dressing rooms, the changing area and they even made a quick pass through the sewing room.

"The sewing room is one of the most important backstage areas. The expensive stage costumes take a beating every day. Tears and rips are a common occurrence." Millie pointed out that because the staff was unable to send the costumes out for repairs, a handful of them were proficient tailors.

"What is the average cost of one of the more elaborate costumes?"

"I once heard some of the more ornate costumes can run in the thousands. The more sequins, beads and detail on the clothing, the more expensive the costume. They're also heavy." Millie carefully removed one of the beaded gowns from the rack and passed it around.

"Wearing this thing would be a workout in itself," one of the women joked.

"Yes. The Siren of the Seas' singers and dancers are here practicing every day for hours at a time." Millie was proud of her co-workers, who kept grueling schedules.

The singers and dancers were not only stage performers, but they also worked double duty, hosting events, particularly the ones up on the lido deck...the poolside parties, hairy legs competitions and even the *Mixmaster* contests.

Although Millie's schedule was virtually nonstop seven days a week, she didn't have nearly the workload as some of the performers.

Their next tour stop was the engine room below deck. One of the ship's engineers shared some basic information on what it took to navigate and operate a ship the size of the Siren of the Seas.

After finishing the tour of the engine room, they headed upstairs to tour the galley. There was only a trace of a burnt odor when she led them inside.

Annette was in the storage room, clipboard in hand. She did a double take when she saw Millie. "Where's Danielle?"

"She and I traded places." Millie turned to her group. "This is Annette Delacroix, the ship's director of food and beverage. We're standing in one of the main galleys, where many of the ship's meals are prepared."

"How much food do you serve in a typical week?" a guest asked.

"It's called provisioning," Annette explained. "During a typical week, passengers consume two thousand pounds of shrimp, ten thousand pounds of chicken and roughly seventy thousand eggs."

"Whew." A man let out a low whistle. "That's a lot of food."

"Yes, it is," Annette agreed. "Preparing all of the meals keeps us busy." She turned to Millie. "Don't forget to take a quick tour of the walk-in coolers on your way out."

"We're heading there now," Millie said.

They wound their way past the workers and gleaming stainless steel counters. It led to a long hallway. At the end were the ship's walk-in coolers.

"The frozen foods are kept in the farthest back freezers. As the food is needed, it's moved forward to begin the thawing process. After thawing, the items are placed in the refrigerated section. By the end of the cruise, the freezers and refrigerators are emptied. On Saturday, the freezers, refrigerators and dry goods storage areas will be replenished, and we start all over again."

After finishing the kitchen tour, she led them below deck to the crew area. Because crew cabins were off limits, Millie slowed to point them out and then made her way to the crew mess hall.

The passengers peered through the windows while Millie explained the crew dining room was open to all ship employees including the ship's officers. "There is also an officer's dining room. I'll point it out when we walk by."

"Does the crew have their own bar and hang out area?" a passenger asked.

"Yes. We're heading there next."

They passed by the officer's dining room before entering the crew's lounge. Millie waited until everyone was inside. "This is where the crew spends their free time socializing in the evenings. As you can see, we have pool tables, ping-pong, video games and even a snack bar."

"The ship's crew is like a large family. We love our jobs." Millie folded her arms. "We understand you've entrusted us with one of the most precious commodities....time, your vacation. We know you could go anywhere else, yet you chose to spend your vacation with us."

Millie ended the tour where it began, and after answering questions, she handed each of them a ball cap and t-shirt. She also gave them a special logoed lanyard and a coupon for a complimentary beverage, redeemable at the specialty coffee shop or any bar on board the ship.

A woman, the last in line, waited until the others left. "It must be romantic being married to the captain of the ship."

"It is," Millie said.

The woman leaned in. "I met Captain Armati on my first day. He's a handsome man. Why...I would keep an eye on him."

Millie chuckled. "Or maybe two," she joked. "Thank you for joining the tour."

After the last passenger left, Millie wandered upstairs to the *Marseille Lounge*. The only person inside was Danielle, who was cleaning up.

"Hey, Danielle, how did it go?"

"It was fine, but that woman…Tracy."

"Yes, that's her name."

"You're never gonna believe what she did."

Chapter 8

"The chick was ticked off when she found out you were no longer hosting the ornament decorating. She started screaming and raising a ruckus. Finally, she stomped out of the lounge."

"What did you say to her?" Millie asked.

"I let her know she wasn't in charge of the entertainment unless her name was Andy Walker." Danielle curled her lip. "Do you have any idea what a pain it was to clean up those teeny tiny ornament pieces?"

"I can only imagine," Millie said. "And I'm sorry I left you with cleaning up the mess she made."

"I would watch out for her if I were you," Danielle advised.

"That's what I'm trying to do," Millie groaned. "The woman is determined to make my life miserable."

"Look on the bright side, we've only got three more days of this cruise, and two of them are port days." Danielle patted her radio. "Give me a holler if she shows up again."

"Thanks, Danielle," Millie said gratefully. "I appreciate the offer. Hopefully, she'll give up and focus on something more productive."

"Like enjoying her vacation."

Despite Danielle's gracious offer, a dark cloud hung over Millie's head the rest of the day. She was certain at any time, Tracy would pop up at her next event, determined to harass her.

Nic was already inside the apartment when she arrived home late that evening. He took one look at his wife's face and said the first thing to come to mind. "You look as if you just ate a sugar-coated jalapeno."

"I wish." Millie slumped into a chair and kicked off her shoes. "I spent half my day worrying about a stalker popping up at one of my events."

Nic frowned. "Someone is stalking you? We need to report him to Patterson."

"Not a male...it's a female passenger and her name is Tracy." Millie briefly explained the incident at *Killer Karaoke*, how the woman was enraged she wasn't able to sing her song because of Andy's comedy show crisis.

Nic interrupted. "What did she want to sing? Not that it makes much difference."

"A Star is Born."

"More like a stalker is born," Nic joked.

His wife was not amused.

"Sorry. Go on."

"Well, after that, she started showing up at my events. The first was bingo followed by the *Heart and Homes* show yesterday where she began heckling me. This morning, it was the ornament decorating activity. She intentionally dropped an ornament on the floor and it shattered into a million tiny pieces."

"I hope you called security." Nic's frown deepened.

"I did one better. I radioed Danielle and we swapped events. I took the behind the scenes tour and she hosted the ornament decorating. Danielle said she threw a fit when she realized I wasn't returning and stomped out of the lounge."

"Have you seen her since?"

"Nope, not that it mattered. I spent the rest of the day paranoid she would show up and start harassing me."

"I'm sorry to hear you had a bad day. On the bright side, at least the cruise is more than halfway over and we still have a couple of port days."

"Danielle said the same thing, plus she offered to swap with me if Tracy showed up again."

Nic pulled out a chair and sat next to his wife. "I'm having my own set of challenges this week. Donovan and Patterson pulled one of the room stewards off the job after guests reported two separate theft incidents on the same deck."

"Gusti on deck ten," Millie said.

"You heard?"

"Yes. Annette offered to let him help out in the kitchen, and he almost set it on fire."

"You're kidding?" Nic leaned back in his chair.

"Maybe I didn't have such a bad day after all. Gusti is having a much worse day, sitting in the holding cell, and accused of theft." Millie told her husband she had a hard time believing Gusti was involved. "Why would Gusti not only steal from two passengers in less than twenty-four hours, but also leave the cabin doors ajar when he was done? I think someone is trying to frame him."

"It could be," Nic agreed. "Gusti has been an employee on board the Siren of the Seas for several years now. We've never received a complaint about him until now."

"Something isn't adding up." Millie rubbed a weary hand across her brow. "I'm too tired to worry about it tonight."

"I'm whupped too." Nic slid out of the chair and held out his hand to help his wife up. "I was thinking it's time for another date day."

"As long as it doesn't involve riding a dune buggy through the dust bowl," Millie joked.

"Aw. It wasn't that bad," Nic grinned. "Admit it...it was fun."

"Yes, it was fun."

"Perfect. I've got another exciting adventure planned in St. Kitts. I took the liberty of asking Andy if you could sneak away for a few hours tomorrow afternoon."

"So soon? I won't have time to mentally prepare myself."

"Precisely. This way, you'll have one less thing to worry about," Nic said. "An added bonus is less time on board to worry about another run in with Tracy."

"I suppose you're right." Millie paused at the top of the stairs to let Scout catch up. "Will you at least give me a hint?"

"Wear some old clothes and bring along a change of clothes."

"Niccolo Armati! We are not going on another dune buggy excursion."

"We're not. I'm teasing. Wear some comfy clothes and perhaps a pair of sneakers."

"How come I never get to plan the excursions?" Millie whined.

"Because you're waiting for our British Isles adventures." Nic gave her a playful pat on the backside. "Now go get ready before Scout hogs the bed and there's no room left for us."

*****

When Millie woke early the next morning and headed to the bathroom, her first thought was of her date day with Nic.

She was looking forward to not worrying about running into Tracy, at least for part of her day. On the flip side, Millie was mildly concerned over the "fun" adventure her husband planned.

The newlyweds shared a lot in common, but their idea of "fun" wasn't one of them. Nic's idea of fun entailed exciting adventures while Millie was the opposite...her idea of the perfect day was a trip to the spa, a food cooking demonstration or even historic ruins tours. Ziplines and dune buggies weren't amongst them.

Millie brewed a pot of coffee while Nic showered. He joined her on her second cup, and they wandered onto the balcony to savor the early morning solitude.

"The calm before the storm." Millie shaded her eyes and squinted at the sun, barely peeking over the horizon.

"I hope not. Here's to an uneventful morning and a memorable afternoon." Nic lifted his cup in salute, his eyes twinkling with mischief.

"I don't like the way you said that."

"I'm teasing." Nic lowered his cup and softly kissed his wife. "I revise my statement to a wonderful day."

"That's better." Millie downed the last of her coffee and reluctantly glanced at her watch. "I better get going. I want to make sure Andy has my afternoon shift covered before I join the morning stretch class in the gym. What time does our fun-filled afternoon adventure begin?"

"Meet me here at twelve-thirty. I promised Andy I would have you back on board the ship by four o'clock to greet the returning passengers."

"I'll be here." Millie gave her husband a quick kiss and rushed out of the apartment. She hustled down the steps and to the backstage where she found Andy inspecting the bulletin board.

"Hey, Andy."

Her boss spun around. "Hello, Millie. I wasn't expecting to see you this early."

"Nic said he convinced you to give me a few hours off this afternoon and I wanted to make sure you were able to cover my schedule."

"I was. Just make sure you're back on board, dressed for work and ready to greet the guests at four o'clock," Andy said. "Annette was here a few minutes ago. She was looking for you."

"I wonder what's up." Millie unclipped her radio and fiddled with the knobs. "My radio is on."

"She didn't tell me. She seemed distracted."

"Uh-oh." Millie pressed the talk button. "Annette, do you copy?"

There was no answer, so Millie tried again. "Annette Delacroix, do you copy?"

Still no answer. "I better head up to the galley to see what's going on." She thanked Andy for covering her shift and then made a beeline for the galley.

Annette was nowhere in sight, and neither was Amit. It struck Millie as odd since one or the other was always working.

Millie approached a kitchen worker. "Have you seen Annette or Amit this morning?"

"They are downstairs, with security."

Millie's breath caught in her throat. "Oh no. Did something happen?"

"I don't know." The woman shook her head. "All I know is Miss Annette, she got a call on the kitchen phone and then she and Amit they leave in a big hurry and tell me they on the way to security."

Millie thanked the young woman and then raced out of the galley. She ran down the hall to the stairs, taking them two at a time until she reached deck two, where Patterson's office and the ship's holding cell were located.

She didn't slow until she reached Patterson's office. Millie gave it a sharp rap and then pushed it open. "Patterson? Anyone in here?"

Oscar, Patterson's right hand-man and second in command, emerged from the back. "Miss Millie."

"Hey, Oscar. I'm looking for Patterson or Annette Delacroix."

"They are in the holding cell."

Millie pressed a hand to her chest. "Patterson arrested Annette?"

Chapter 9

"No. Patterson is detaining one of the crew for a...guest related incident."

"Gusti," Millie prompted.

"Yes. Gusti. He is talking crazy talk."

"Patterson or Gusti?"

"Gusti, he is the one talking crazy," Oscar said. "Amit and Annette, along with Patterson are trying to calm him down."

Millie thanked Oscar for the information before darting out of the office and down the hall to the holding cell. She could hear muffled voices coming from within.

One of the voices belonged to Annette. Millie eased the door open and stepped inside where she found Amit, Annette and Patterson huddled around a visibly upset Gusti.

"But this is the end for me. My career is over. I cannot return to my country with this shame. It would be better for me if I jump over the side of the ship and end it all."

"Gusti, don't keep saying that," Patterson replied. "I'm keeping you here for your own good. You are safe. No one has accused you of a crime."

"But you pull me off my job and send me to the galley. It might as well have been the gallows. I set the kitchen on fire." Gusti's face crumpled. "I am a miserable failure. I don't blame you for locking me up."

Millie's heart went out to the poor man. "I'm sorry to interrupt. Gusti, Patterson is right. He's only keeping you for your own good. Besides, you didn't technically set the kitchen on fire. It was just a little...smoky."

She could see Gusti was listening, so she pressed on. "I probably would've done the same thing. It's only a matter of time before Patterson clears your name and you're free to return to your job."

The words rang hollow in Millie's ears. What if Gusti was guilty? Maybe he was consumed with guilt after being caught and was contemplating taking his own life instead of being sent to prison.

She quickly dismissed the idea. The fact Gusti worked on board the ship for several years without incident should be enough proof the man was innocent. Surely, there was another explanation for the coincidence of the thefts on deck ten.

Annette's radio squawked. It was one of the kitchen staff. "Miss Annette. Do you copy?"

"It's Grace." Annette lifted her radio. "Go ahead, Grace."

"We have a minor emergency in the galley. The line cook is refusing to serve the stuffed French toast. He's insisting it tastes like tofu."

"I'll be right there." Annette replaced her radio. "Gusti, keep your chin up. If you need to come back to the kitchen, you're welcome anytime." She patted the man on the shoulder and exited the holding cell.

"I must get back to work, too. I will check on you later," Amit promised his friend before following Annette out, leaving Patterson and Millie alone with Gusti.

Patterson gave Millie a helpless look.

Millie knelt down and placed a light hand on Gusti's arm. "Gusti, we know you're distraught. Have faith in Patterson. He'll get to the bottom of this and the truth will come out."

Gusti lifted his head, his sorrowful eyes meeting Millie's. "But what if it doesn't?" he whispered. "This cloud of suspicion...it will always hang over my head."

"No, it won't." Millie shook her head. "Patterson is good. He'll get to the bottom of what happened to the guests' missing items."

She started to stand and had a sudden thought. "Would you like me to pray with you?"

An unreadable expression flitted across Gusti's face, and he nodded. "Yes. I need all of the prayers I can get."

Millie reached for his hands and bowed her head. "Dear Heavenly Father. I bring my friend, Gusti, to you in prayer this morning. His heart is heavy because of the recent incidents on board the ship. Lord, we ask you to clear Gusti's good name quickly and that the real perpetrators, the person or persons responsible for these shameful crimes against others, be caught and brought to justice. I ask for peace in Gusti's heart and thank you for hearing our heartfelt prayer."

Millie gave Gusti's hands a squeeze before lifting her head. She caught a glimpse of him swiping at his eyes. "It will be okay, Gusti."

"Thank you, Millie." Patterson said softly.

"I feel better, Miss Millie." Gusti attempted a smile. "Do not worry. I will trust God. He will help Mr. Patterson to find the truth."

"Good. In the meantime, enjoy a little time off. Perhaps Patterson can arrange for a television or some books to be brought down to help pass the time."

"Yes, it can be arranged," Patterson quickly agreed. "As I said, until we clear your name, this is only a precaution."

The trio chatted for several more moments until Millie was certain Gusti would not try to harm himself. He seemed to brighten at the prospect of having a television or books brought in.

Millie stepped into the hall and waited for Patterson, who joined her moments later. "You will try to make Gusti a little more comfortable."

"Yes, as soon as I get back to my office, I'll ask maintenance to bring Gusti a television, a laptop and then I'll have room service bring some snacks and food. By the time we're done, he's going to be begging to stay in confinement."

"I'm sure he won't." Millie smiled. "How is your investigation going?"

"It's not. The only thing certain is both thefts occurred on the same deck. Both cabins were broken into at night while the passengers were out, and both were missing money."

"Money?" Millie lifted a brow. "Is that it?"

"No." Patterson shook his head. "The second theft victim claims he's missing an expensive wristwatch, as well. I'm waiting for both of them to finish filling out an incident report."

"And there are no cameras in the hall to capture who the perpetrators may have been," Millie said.

"Unfortunately, no. The keycard monitoring system shows no unusual activity, either, which is puzzling." Patterson started to say something else and then stopped.

"Which means Gusti's keycard isn't showing he accessed the cabins, either?" Millie asked.

"Correct. We have records of the turndown service in the early evening, around dinnertime and then nothing. Only the passengers' cards were used, the ones who occupy the cabins."

"Odd," Millie murmured. "So what happens next?"

"I wait until the passengers turn in the incident reports and then forward them to corporate. Since Gusti has never been accused before and we have no proof or record he was even near the cabins at the time of the thefts, corporate will settle the claims if nothing else happens. End of story."

"But cash? How do you compensate a passenger when they claim cash was stolen?" Millie asked.

"I leave that up to the lawyers to hammer out," Patterson said. "My job is to report what happened. They're the ones who work out the compensation."

"You're sure as long as nothing else happens, Gusti is in the clear?" Millie asked.

"I hope so. Look…" Patterson rocked back on his heels as he studied Millie's face. "I can see the wheels spinning in your head. We have two incidents, although not necessarily isolated. Gusti is safe for now. I didn't want to upset him even more, but I may not put him back on the floor until the end of this cruise for his own protection."

"You'll send him back to Annette's gallows?" Millie joked.

Patterson cracked a smile. "Better him working for Delacroix than me."

Millie waved dismissively. "Annette's bark is worse than her bite." She turned to go.

"Hey, Millie."

Millie turned back. "Yeah?"

"Thanks." Patterson pointed to the holding cell. "Thanks for praying with Gusti."

"You're welcome. We can all use a little divine intervention in a time of need. You should try it sometime."

"Maybe I will."

Before Millie left, she reminded Patterson about his promise to Gusti and then headed upstairs.

The *Waves Buffet* was a madhouse with guests crowding in around the food stations to fill up on breakfast before heading out for their day on the beautiful island of St. Kitts.

Instead of fighting the crowds, Millie grabbed a banana and a box of cold cereal. There wasn't an empty seat in the place, so she headed to the back of the ship and a quiet corner most of the passengers rarely visited.

The alcove faced the island's port and offered a view of the docking post along with a long line of tour buses.

Millie prayed over her food, adding another prayer for Gusti and that the real thief or thieves would be caught.

While she ate, she thought of the young woman, Amy, she met the previous morning, the one whose cabin was next door to the second theft victim.

Patterson didn't appear to have a lot of information on either of the thefts or exactly what had been stolen. Perhaps the guests knew they were missing cash, but couldn't recall an exact amount.

Amy mentioned to Millie that she and her sister were early birds, and Millie decided it wouldn't hurt to stop by the young woman's cabin to see if she'd heard anything else.

Millie finished her food and headed down to guest services.

Nikki Tan was working the desk, and she motioned Millie over. "Hello, Millie. You look chipper this morning."

"Good morning, Nikki. I need a favor. I was wondering if you could take a quick look at your guest log."

"Of course." Nikki reached for the mouse. "Who are you trying to track down?"

"The passenger's name is Amy. She and her sister are in a cabin on deck ten."

"Ah. Yes. Amy Markowski. She shares a cabin with a Carley Markowski."

"Perfect. What is Amy's cabin number?"

"Cabin ten, six six one."

"Could you please jot the cabin number on a sheet of paper? I'm terrible at remembering numbers."

Nikki jotted the number down and handed the slip of paper to Millie.

"Thank you, Nikki."

"You're welcome. This wouldn't happen to have anything to do with the recent thefts on deck ten, would it?"

"Maybe. You know me," Millie folded the paper. "Poor Gusti is beside himself since he was the cabin steward for both of these passengers."

"Gusti has been on board longer than me," Nikki said. "I don't think he's responsible."

"Me, either, which is why I'm going to do a little nosing around." Millie thanked Nikki again and then headed to the gym for the sunrise stretch.

The stretching class dragged by and Millie wondered if it would ever end. Finally, it was time to roll up her mat, and she flew out the door.

The side stairs were the quickest route to deck ten. She picked up the pace as she power-walked to the other end of the ship; the door of cabin ten, six six one sported a festive palm tree cutout.

Millie lifted a hand and then hesitated. What if Amy and her sister were still asleep? Gusti's forlorn face popped into Millie's head, settling her internal debate.

There was a muffled noise after Millie's light knock. The door opened, and a young woman who bore a resemblance to Amy appeared in the doorway.

"Hello. My name is Millie Armati. I'm the assistant cruise director. I met your sister, Amy, yesterday. I was wondering if she's around."

"Yeah." The door opened wider as the woman turned. "Amy, it's for you."

Amy popped into view. She smiled when she recognized Millie. "Hello, Millie. I missed you and Scout this morning at the sunrise stride."

"We missed you, too. It was my turn to co-host the sunrise *stretch* this morning, not the stride." Millie got right to the point. "Yesterday, you mentioned your next door neighbor's theft, and I was wondering if I could ask you a couple more questions."

"We've already talked to a man named Patterson," Carley interrupted.

"I'm not technically working with Mr. Patterson, the head of security. I'm here on my own, to try to help a friend."

"Gusti?" Amy asked.

"Yes. Gusti. I was hoping maybe you remembered or found out a little more about the incident next door."

"As a matter of fact..." Amy motioned Millie into the cabin and quietly closed the door behind her.

Chapter 10

"The couple was arguing something fierce last night." Amy jabbed her finger in the direction of the cabin next door. "We couldn't hear what they were saying. They were really going at it, weren't they Carley?"

"Yeah. It was kinda scary. We thought about calling security, but figured they would know we were the ones who turned them in. Before we could decide what to do, one of them slammed the door. It slammed so hard, it shook our television and then it got quiet. I guess they left," Amy added.

"But you couldn't hear what they were arguing about?"

"No. We even snuck out onto our balcony thinking one of them might go outside," Amy said.

"Have you talked to them since the theft?"

"We ran into them in the hall yesterday afternoon and asked them about it. They said they were missing some cash and a watch that was on the desk."

"I hate to sound nosy, but did they say how much cash?" Millie asked.

Amy and Carley exchanged a quick glance. "Close to a thousand dollars."

Millie lifted a brow. "A thousand dollars? That's a nice chunk of change to have on board considering the Siren of the Seas is a cashless system. Most expenses are put on a shipboard charge account."

She asked the sisters a couple more questions. Other than the argument and a rough estimate of the amount of money the passengers claimed was missing, the sisters didn't know much else.

"Thank you for your time." Millie changed the subject. "Are you doing anything fun in St. Kitts?"

"Oh yes." Carley nodded enthusiastically. "We signed up for a dune buggy island tour. It's the number one rated activity on St. Kitts."

"Wear old clothes and bring a change of clothes, not to mention sunscreen," Millie advised.

Amy's mouth fell open. "You've taken the dune buggy tour?"

"Yes. A couple of months ago, the captain surprised me with a dune buggy excursion. If you booked through the St. Kitts Dune Buggy Company, you can count on a wild adventure."

Carley wrinkled her nose. "I heard we'll get dirty, like really dirty."

"They'll give you a bandana to cover your face, so you don't breathe in the dust."

The young woman looked horrified.

Millie patted her arm. "Don't worry. The views are spectacular. The hosts will keep you safe. Just be sure to take lots of pictures...and a change of clothes."

"Amy." Carley stared accusingly at her sister. "What have you gotten us into?"

Millie took this as her cue to make a hasty exit. She thanked them again for taking the time to answer some questions.

After exiting the cabin, Millie slowly walked past the cabin next door. The cruise line allowed passengers to secure an onboard account using a cash deposit, although most passengers used a credit card instead. Proving a cash loss would be tricky. Convincing Majestic Cruise Lines to compensate them for the alleged loss would be even trickier.

It was a problem Millie was glad didn't involve her.

It was time to head to the casino to host her first ever Christmas matchup contest. As she suspected, there were only a handful of participants...perfect for trying out a new activity.

Millie handed out copies of the riddles, briefly explaining the participants would have fifteen minutes to match the questions to the answers, or until someone was the first to complete them all.

"Ready, set, go!" She set her watch and then wandered over to the window to check the weather. It was going to be a beautiful day. The sun was shining, and there was a slight ripple on the water, meaning the port area was enjoying a nice breeze.

Her thoughts drifted to Gusti and the thefts. By now, Patterson would have delivered some of the creature comforts to the ship's employee.

The more Millie mulled over the situation, the more she was convinced Gusti was not involved in the thefts. He had zero history of past disciplinary matters, not to mention no one would be dumb enough to steal from two of their assigned cabins on the same deck no less and then leave the doors ajar.

"I'm done." One of the guests triumphantly waved the questionnaire in the air and Millie hurried to his side. She scanned the sheet to verify the man had filled in all of the blanks.

"It looks like we may have a winner." A few groans went up, and Millie grabbed her answer sheet before slipping her reading glasses on.

She made her way down the list and discovered the contestant mixed up two of the answers.

Despite the mix-up, the man still managed to match the most answers. Millie presented him with a coupon for the *Sprinkles* ice cream shop and a ship on a stick.

"I'll be hosting our regular round of trivia later this afternoon, right here if you would like to join me." She thanked the departing participants and then headed back to the apartment.

Nic wasn't on the bridge. First Officer Craig McMasters told her he'd left and was on his way to the gangway after a brief meeting with Dave Patterson.

"Thanks for the heads up." Millie darted inside the apartment and found Scout waiting on the other side of the door. She let her pooch out and checked his food and water dishes before making her way upstairs to change.

Nic suggested cool, comfortable clothes and comfortable shoes. Millie chose a light pink button down blouse and a pair of khaki Bermuda shorts. She reached for her favorite sandals, but at the last minute opted to go with a pair of sneakers.

Before she left, she grabbed her ship logoed mini backpack and tossed in a bottle of sunscreen. On her way out, she slipped her sunglasses on her head and added some bottled waters to the backpack.

The Siren of the Seas docked mid-morning, and most of the passengers with early excursions had exited the ship hours ago. Despite the casual clothing, Millie was certain several of the ship's crewmembers and even a couple of the passengers recognized her.

She "dinged" her keycard and strolled down the gangway.

A strong gust of wind lifted the corners of her hair and blew the strands across her eyes. Millie impatiently pushed them aside as she scanned the crowd, searching for her husband.

He was nowhere in sight, so she stepped off to the side to make a couple of calls. Millie dialed her son, Blake's cell phone, ready to leave him a brief message. Much to her surprise, he picked up.

"You got my message?"

"No, son. We've been at sea for a couple of days, and my phone was turned off. I just turned it back on. I'm standing on the dock in St. Kitts waiting for Nic."

"You haven't talked to Beth?"

"Not yet. Is everything all right?"

"There's been a small accident."

Chapter 11

Blake hurried on. "It's about Beth. She was involved in an automobile accident. Her car is totaled. She, Noah and Bella are fine."

"Fine?" Millie's legs threatened to give way, and she reached out to steady herself. "Beth's car is totaled, yet she and the kids are fine?"

"I knew I should've let Beth talk to you first."

"No." Millie fought to remain calm. "Someone should've called the ship's emergency number to let me know what happened."

"Mom, please. Everything is fine. I shouldn't have said anything."

"Blake, you're only making matters worse."

"I think you're right," Blake said miserably. "Look, call Beth's cell phone. She's home now."

"I will. I'm sorry if I yelled. I'm just freaked out."

Millie told her son she loved him before ending the call. Her hands shook as she dialed her daughter's cell phone.

She didn't notice Nic quietly make his way over. "What's going on?"

"There's been an accident." Millie's lower lip trembled, and she rambled as she tried to tell her husband that Beth and her grandchildren had been involved in an accident.

The call rang through. "Mom?"

"Beth. I talked to Blake. He said you and the kids were involved in a car accident."

"We're fine. Another car blew through a red light. They ran into the back of our car and spun us around. We're a little shaken, but otherwise fine."

Millie pressed a hand to her chest. "Thank you, Jesus."

Beth continued. "The car wasn't quite as lucky. I think it's totaled, at least that's what Dad said."

"Your father is with you?"

"David is out of town. I asked Dad to meet us at the hospital. He was throwing a fit, and they almost threw him out."

"That sounds about right," Millie said.

"I asked Blake to call you to let you know."

"He said he left a message on my cell phone, but my cell phone was turned off. Next time, call the ship's security number," Millie scolded.

"We would have, but again it was a minor accident. We'll be fine."

Millie tilted the phone away from her face. "Beth and the kids were involved in an accident. Someone blew through a red light and hit the back of their car. Although the car is in rough shape, they're all okay."

Millie shifted the phone. "Nic is with me. I told him what happened."

"David is calling," Beth said. "I'll call you back a little later."

"Okay." Millie told her daughter that she loved her, and with tears in her eyes disconnected the line. "It could've been so bad."

"But it wasn't." Nic slipped his arms around his wife, and Millie placed her head against his chest.

A tear trickled down her cheek at the thought of what could have happened. She silently thanked God for protecting her children and grandchildren.

Nic promised they would not get back on board the ship until she was able to talk to Beth again.

Millie drew a shaky breath and pulled away. "Thank you. We better get going, or we're going to be late."

"We won't be late. I booked a private excursion. It's just the two of us. We're meeting our guides at the end of the dock." Nic reached for his wife's hand. They began walking toward the pavilion where several of the tour guides stood waving large placards.

"Which one is ours?" Millie's eyes scanned the crowd.

"Over there." Nic pointed to a woman standing near a row of empty benches.

"Where?" Millie stopped in her tracks when she read the woman's sign. "You're kidding."

*****

"No," Nic beamed. "This is it."

"Seriously. Tell me we're not taking a Segway tour."

"We're not taking a Segway tour." Nic led his wife toward the woman. "Armati, party of two."

"Yes. Captain Armati. I was beginning to wonder if you were going to make it."

"There's been a small family emergency. I think we're good to go now." Nic turned to his wife. "Millie?"

"Segways?" Millie took a step back. "I've never been on a Segway. This is almost worse than a dune buggy. At least I wasn't driving."

"You won't be driving, Mum," the woman said. "You'll be steering. Don't worry. You'll be in good hands with Victor and Melvin."

Millie's eyes narrowed accusingly. "You tricked me."

"How did I trick you?" Nic argued.

The woman motioned them to follow her through a courtyard, to the end of the street where they met another man, Victor, according to his nametag. "Victor will take over from here."

"It's going to be a beautiful day for a Segway tour," Victor said. "Follow me."

They walked past several gift shops and restaurants, before turning the corner and crossing over a circular brick parking area.

Lined up off to one side were four Segways.

"Have you ever ridden Segways before?" Victor asked.

"No." Nic rubbed his hands together. "One of the other crewmembers on board our ship recommended your company. He said he had a terrific time on your tour."

"It wouldn't happen to have been Vitale again, would it?" Millie asked.

"Yes, as a matter of fact, it was Antonio. How did you know?"

"Because Antonio *also* recommended the dune buggy excursion. I'm going to have a chat with him when we get back to the ship."

"C'mon," Nic cajoled. "You're already complaining, and you haven't even tried it yet."

"We must fill out some paperwork before we begin." Melvin, the other tour guide, handed Millie and Nic each a clipboard and an ink pen.

Millie breezed over the disclaimer. It waived the tour company from any responsibility in the event she was injured. She signed and dated the disclaimer and then handed it back to Melvin.

"We'll start with you." Victor steered one of the Segways out of the portico and parked it in front of Millie. "It's as easy as riding a bike."

"I haven't ridden a bike in years."

Victor ignored the comment as he lifted a helmet off the handlebars and placed it on top of Millie's head before adjusting the strap. "Safety first." He tugged on the strap to tighten it.

"Perfect. Now you." He helped Nic with his helmet before placing his own on his head. Melvin, the other guide, watched as Victor showed the couple how to operate the Segway.

"Place your feet on the center of each footrest. To go forward, lean forward on the platform. To go backward, lightly press down with the back of your heel. To go left, ease the handle to the left. To go right, gently steer the handle to the right."

"Where's the brake?" Millie asked.

"There is no brake, Mum. To stop, balance your feet on the center."

"There's no brake?" Millie gasped. "What if I need to make a sudden stop?"

"Then you'll need to level your feet as quickly as possible."

Millie wrinkled her nose. "I don't know about this. This is an accident waiting to happen."

"You will be fine." Victor patted the front of the Segway. "I will help you get on, and then you can practice by riding around here."

Nic was grinning from ear-to-ear as he hopped on the Segway. He eased it forward and then eased it back. He looped around the circular drive, a look of excitement on his face as he breezed by Millie.

"You must at least try," Victor urged.

Not wanting to disappoint her husband, Millie reluctantly climbed on the Segway. She inched forward, centering each foot on the sides of the platform and reached for the handle.

"We'll go slowly. Press lightly on the front of the platform."

Millie followed Victor's instructions; applying a small amount of pressure to the front of the platform.

The Segway coasted forward.

"You're doing good," Victor said. "Now press a little harder."

Millie pressed a little harder, and the Segway picked up speed...more speed than she'd anticipated.

She let out a yelp, her heart pounding as she attempted to slow the contraption. In a panic, she pressed down hard with her toes. The Segway picked up even more speed.

"You might want to ease off." Victor made a desperate grab for the Segway's handlebars, but it was moving too fast.

"I can't! This thing is out of control!" Millie gripped the handlebars, desperately willing the Segway to stop. The harder she tried, the faster she went. "Help!"

Victor ran after Millie and her runaway Segway.

Melvin raced across the drive, coming at her from the opposite direction. He lunged forward, grabbing the handlebars mere seconds before the Segway plowed full speed into the curb.

The sudden movement caused Millie to lose her footing. Her arms flailed in the air as she fell backward, right into Victor's arms.

"Umpf." Her helmet flew forward, covering her eyes and blocking her vision.

"You okay, Mum?" Victor stood her upright.

"I...the Segway just went crazy. I couldn't control it."

"You panicked and pressed too hard on the front of the platform instead of evening out the pressure, causing you to pick up speed," Melvin explained.

"I did?"

"Yes." Victor gave Millie's shoulder a reassuring squeeze before releasing his grip. "It's a common first time mistake."

Nic sped across the drive. He hopped off the Segway and ran to his wife's side. "Millie, are you all right?"

"I'm fine, now that both feet are firmly planted on the ground," Millie snapped.

Nic's expression sobered at the sharp tone in his wife's voice.

A wave of guilt washed over Millie. "I'm sorry. I'm just a little stressed out. Maybe Segways aren't my cup of tea."

"Maybe not." Nic removed his helmet.

Victor, anxious to smooth things over, held up his hand. "Like I said, it is a common first time mistake. Millie knows not to press too hard on the front of the platform. We can try again."

What Millie really wanted to do was hand her helmet to Victor and head back to the ship, but then she would be admitting defeat, something she detested.

Instead, she squared her shoulders. "Victor is right. I panicked. I know not to press too hard. I'm ready to try again."

"Good girl," Nic brightened. "I know you can do it."

Melvin helped Millie climb back on the Segway. "Remember, pressing too hard with your heel will have the same effect, except in reverse and nobody wants to speed backwards on a Segway."

"And definitely not me." Millie wiped her sweaty palms on the front of her shorts, determined not to let the Segway ruin her day.

This time, she was mindful not to press too hard. She circled the brick parking area several times.

Victor clapped his hands as Millie made her fourth pass, a smile on her face.

"You got this, girl."

"I believe I finally do." Millie eased back, and the Segway rolled to a stop. "I think I'm ready."

"I think you are, too." Victor explained they would ride out of town, making their way along the bay area. "Our first stop is a magnificent overlook with the Siren of the Seas in the background."

The first few minutes of riding was a slow go for Millie, but at least she was doing it. She managed to navigate her way over a bridge, dodging several pedestrians and even crossed the street before they reached the overlook.

"We will take your picture if you like," Melvin offered.

"That would be great." Nic pulled his cell phone from his front pocket, switched it on and then handed it to Melvin while Victor steered their Segways closer together for the photo op.

He took several pictures. Melvin handed the cell phone back, and they continued the Segway tour. The more Millie rode, the more comfortable she became at navigating the Segway.

Palm Court Gardens was the next stop. Victor helped the couple step off their Segways and guided them inside the courtyard and the lush tropical paradise.

The gardens tour started near the entrance where Melvin pointed out the various herbs and trees. Millie was particularly enthralled with the soursop tree, a broadleaf, flowering, evergreen tree native to the tropical region.

He plucked one of the long, prickly fruits from the tree and handed it to Millie. "The soursop is also known as custard apple. Practitioners of herbal medicine use soursop fruit and graviola tree leaves to treat stomach ailments, fever, parasitic infections, hypertension and rheumatism. It's used as a sedative, as well."

Millie inspected the fruit before passing it to Nic. "What does it taste like?"

"Although the name suggests it is sour, some pieces are both sweet and sour, while others are very sweet. The flavor is a combination of pineapple and banana or papaya."

Basil, lemongrass and an herb that reminded Millie of licorice were all a part of the tour.

After finishing the garden tour, Melvin and Victor encouraged Nic and Millie to explore the terrace, the courtyard, the pool area and the rooftop deck to enjoy the scenery and snap more pictures.

Nic waited until they were out of earshot. "You got the hang of the Segway. For a few minutes though..." He shook his head.

"For a few minutes, I wanted to throttle you," Millie joked. "You would've felt terrible if I had gotten hurt."

"You're right, and I'm sorry. I didn't think it would be as tricky as it was. Next time, I'll let you pick the excursion." Nic slipped his arm around his wife's waist and then held up his phone to snap some selfies.

They stayed on the rooftop deck as long as they dared before joining their tour guides at the front to resume the rest of the Segway tour.

Next on the tour was a brief stop in the historical Fortlands area and a visit to the War Memorial before they began the trek back to Port Zante, their starting point.

Millie spent the return trip focusing on making sure she kept her feet evenly spaced. When they reached the brick parking area, her legs wobbled as she climbed off the Segway's platform.

Although she enjoyed the tour, the gardens and the memorials, she was relieved to have both feet firmly planted on solid ground.

"Thank you for a fun afternoon." Nic shook Victor and Melvin's hands and handed each of them a generous tip.

"Thank you for saving my life." Millie joined her husband and shook Victor's hand.

"Millie, you are a real trooper. I thought you weren't gonna get back on the Segway after the near collision with the curb."

"And I almost didn't," Millie replied.

"But you did good."

"And I thoroughly enjoyed the tour."

The couple began making their way back to the center square and main touristy area.

"I found the perfect surprise stop off for lunch," Nic said.

"Another surprise?" Millie asked.

"Yes, but a good one."

Millie wasn't convinced. "We'll see about that."

Chapter 12

Nic consulted his cell phone when they reached the corner. The couple turned left, walking in the opposite direction of the port and ship.

"This is it." He stopped in front of the *Port Zante Grill* where he and Millie perused the menu posted near the entrance.

"The *Taste of Caribbean* menu sounds intriguing," Millie said. "It includes spicy jerk chicken with rice and vegetables."

"I may try the *Port Zante Plate,*" Nic said.

Millie rattled off the description. "A collection of sliced sashimi yellowfin tuna, chilled garlic shrimps, grilled fish and veggies, olives, seaweed, ginger, oriental dips and salsa with garlic bread. That's a lot of food."

"I think I can handle it, plus we can share."

"The seaweed is all yours," Millie teased.

Nic held the door for his wife, and Millie stepped inside.

The cooler air was a welcome relief from the humid outdoors. The beat of steel drums drifted in through the courtyard's open doors in the back.

The couple ordered their food, and while they waited, they began reliving their Segway adventure. All the while, Beth's accident was in the back of Millie's mind.

"Are you all right? You seem distracted."

"I'm worried about Beth and the kids," Millie said.

"Why don't you give them a call while we wait for our food?"

"That's a great idea." Millie dialed her daughter's cell phone, and Beth answered, sounding a little less stressed.

She reassured her mother again that everyone was all right and David was on his way home.

Beth shifted the conversation away from the accident, and they discussed Millie and Nic's Segway adventure, the upcoming holidays, which wouldn't include a visit from her children and grandchildren this year.

"It's sad we won't be together." Millie could feel herself getting teary-eyed at the thought of not being with her children and grandchildren for Christmas.

"But we'll see you in the spring when you come home before heading to the other side of the world," Beth teased.

"It's not the other side of the world. Just the other side of the ocean." A thought occurred to Millie. "What if you, David and the kids cruised the British Isles with us next summer?"

"That would be fun." Beth was quiet for a moment. "I could run it by David, to see what he thinks."

Millie quickly warmed to the idea. "I'm sure there are still some open cabins. If you think it's something you might do, Nic can request the cruise line hold a cabin for you."

"Don't do anything yet," Beth warned. "Let me ask first. I'll let you know what he says when we talk again on Saturday." Before Beth hung up, Millie chatted with her grandchildren, and then the phone went back to Beth before saying good-bye.

Nic watched his wife slip the cell phone inside her backpack. "Do you feel better now?"

"Much better."

"Good." Nic reached across the table and grabbed Millie's hand. "I have a wonderful life and a wonderful wife."

Millie's heart fluttered. "I feel the same. God has truly blessed me with the most wonderful husband ever."

The food arrived, ending their tender moment. The server shifted Millie's plate of chicken and rice from the tray to the table before placing Nic's large platter of food in front of him. There were also two smaller side dishes.

"I'm starving." Nic leaned in to take a whiff. "It smells delicious."

Millie smoothed her napkin across her lap. "It's hard to believe Christmas is right around the corner. It sure doesn't feel like it."

"I agree." Nic asked his wife for details on Andy's Christmas theme, and finally, the topic turned to the unsettling thefts on deck ten.

"What do you think happened?" Nic stabbed one of his shrimp with his fork.

"I don't think Gusti is responsible for the thefts. Think about it...he's been on board the Siren of the

Seas for several years without a single reprimand or write up. There's no way he would risk losing his job over cash."

She told Nic how he'd been depressed and how she prayed with him. "I'm hoping by the time we get back to the ship, Patterson will clear Gusti and let him return to work."

"It may not be possible," Nic warned. "If the passengers suspect Gusti of stealing from them, they won't want him inside their cabins. I'm sure we can find another spot for him until this group of passengers disembarks."

"Annette invited him to work in the kitchen. Gusti nearly set it on fire." Millie briefly told him about the bubbling food and Annette freaking out.

"Oh dear. I hadn't heard that. I'll track down Donovan Sweeney to see if we can place him somewhere else."

"Could you? I would hate to know Gusti will be sitting in the holding cell for two more days."

Their time together flew by and too soon, the meal ended and it was time to return to the ship.

Nic paid the bill while Millie gathered their belongings.

They exited the restaurant where large storm clouds gathered overhead. Thunder rumbled, and Millie eyed the clouds warily. "I think we're in for a downpour."

The couple picked up the pace and jogged through town, to the pier where the ship was docked. They made it all the way to the gangway before the skies let loose.

Warm rain pelted Millie's bare arms, her shoulders and the top of her head. By the time the couple cleared security, both Nic and she were soaking wet.

Millie shivered as the ship's air conditioning blasted cold air on her. "An exciting finale to an exciting day."

"You can never accuse me of being boring."

"You got that right."

They climbed the stairs to the bridge, where they passed through on their way to their apartment.

Scout greeted them at the door.

"We're back." Millie grabbed a dishtowel to dry her arms before letting Scout out on the balcony. Since Nic needed to report to the bridge before Millie started her shift, they agreed he would get ready first.

Although the balcony was covered, the pup didn't care for the rumbling thunder and occasional bolt of lightning off in the distance. Scout made quick work of taking care of business before scampering back inside.

Nic returned downstairs a short time later, dressed in uniform.

Millie let out a low whistle. "What a lucky woman I am."

"Not as lucky or blessed as me." Nic playfully tugged on a wet strand of his wife's hair. "You look like a drowned rat."

"Thanks to you."

Nic's eyes darkened. "Our date day ended too soon. How does a romantic dinner for two sound?"

Millie lowered her eyelids. "I love the idea. I'm off at eleven."

"Antonio takes over on the bridge at ten-thirty. I'll order room service, and we can eat in. What sounds good?"

"Something light. I could go for a fresh salad and maybe grilled chicken or grilled fish."

"Fish?" Nic chuckled. "There was fish on my plate at lunch, and you refused to try a single bite."

"That's because they brought the fish out whole, fins and all...and it was staring at me."

"It was not staring at you."

"It was. Anyway, fish or chicken. Surprise me." Millie bounced on her tiptoes to kiss her handsome husband.

After Nic left, Millie peeled off her wet clothes and stepped into the hot shower, letting the water warm her body. While she scrubbed, she thought about Gusti and prayed he was still in good spirits.

She finished showering and toweled off before running a quick comb through her hair to smooth it into a tight ponytail. Millie topped off her new "do" with a loose twist.

She slipped into a crisp, clean uniform, and after a quick inspection in the mirror, exited the apartment.

Millie beat Andy to the gangway to greet the returning guests. He arrived moments later, an aggravated expression on his face.

"You look like you ate sour grapes."

"Sour grapes are an understatement. It's been a challenging day on board the ship, to say the least."

"Challenging day? What happened?"

"I met with Donovan Sweeney and Dave Patterson. Another passenger reported a theft."

Chapter 13

"Please tell me it wasn't another cabin break in on deck ten."

"No. This one occurred on the lido deck."

"The lido deck...in broad daylight?"

Andy told Millie a woman left her beach bag and other personal belongings on a lounge chair while she grabbed a bite to eat in the buffet. When she returned a short time later, her belongings were gone.

"Poof? Disappeared?" Millie snapped her fingers. "Maybe it was a chair hog incident, another passenger or passengers got fed up and turned her stuff in to the ship's staff."

A common problem and complaint among cruise ship passengers was when fellow passengers would head up to the lido deck early in the morning, place beach towels and other belongings on the chairs to save them, then returning at their leisure, and successfully snagging a prime location near the pool or outdoor buffet areas for the entire day.

The ship's official policy was if the items remained unclaimed for more than an hour, fellow passengers were allowed to remove the belongings from the saved lounge chairs and turn them in to the ship's staff, so others could use the chairs.

Unfortunately, the policy caused conflict with the passengers and confrontations on the lido deck were regular occurrences.

It was a hot topic, and one Majestic struggled with since handling passengers' personal belongings put them at risk for complaints of theft...a perfect example of what Andy was describing.

"Well, therein lies another problem. The items were turned in to the ship's staff. The passenger was able to get her items back...minus some valuables."

"What sort of valuables?" Millie asked.

"She claims she's missing a small amount of cash, an iPad and an expensive pair of earrings."

"The passenger should not have left valuable items unattended. They're only inviting someone to steal the stuff."

"I agree." Andy sighed heavily. "Unfortunately, passengers don't necessarily see it that way."

Millie eyed her boss thoughtfully. "Perhaps they got the thief on camera. There are cameras on the lido deck."

"Patterson's staff is reviewing the surveillance camera's footage. We both know how many people are on board this ship, how many passengers pass through the lido area and interact with the ship's staff. It will be like looking for a needle in a haystack."

"That's terrible. I guess it's time to remind guests not to leave items unattended anywhere on board the ship."

A group of passengers boarded the ship, interrupting their conversation to ask what time the buffet stopped serving lunch.

Andy answered their question and waited for them to walk away. "There has been another theft just as disturbing."

"You're kidding."

"I went over your reindeer hiding locations to check them myself, and one of them is missing."

Millie snorted. "Someone stole one of the reindeer?"

"It was the little guy you stuck in the window of *Sprinkles*, the ice cream and candy shop, right next to the birthday cake display."

"Maybe one of the junior passengers liked the reindeer so much, they decided to take him home," Millie teased.

"It could be. The loss means we're down to only forty-nine reindeer for our contest. I've decided to order another dozen, to keep for extras in case more come up missing during the holiday season."

Millie started to reply but knew no amount of reasoning would stop Andy from his reindeer games.

"Check it out." She pointed to the dock where sheets of rain poured down. It was raining so hard, Millie struggled to see the end of the gangway.

The rain let up, and passengers resumed boarding. In between greeting the returning passengers, Millie thought about the thefts. It was possible the cabin thefts on deck ten and the missing items on the lido deck were unrelated.

A cruise ship was no more dangerous...or no safer than any land-based vacation. She knew from previous experience cruise ship passengers tended to let their guard down once they boarded the ship and slipped into vacation-mode.

Millie thought back to all of the crimes committed on board the Siren of the Seas since she joined the staff...poisonings, murder, Cat's kidnapping, even an attempted hijacking of the cruise ship. They ran the gamut, and if this cruise was any indication, there was no sign of it letting up.

Of course, there were thousands of passengers on board the ship at any given time, bringing with them personal issues, family feuds and jealousy, not to mention criminal activity and the list went on.

After the last guest boarded, Suharto and the boarding crew removed the gangway, and the ship set sail.

Millie headed down to Patterson's office to check on Gusti. Instead of Oscar this time, Patterson was in his office. He waved Millie inside and waited for her to close the door. "You're here to check on Gusti."

"Yep. Is he still in the holding cell?"

Patterson folded his hands and leaned back in the chair. "Yes. Unfortunately, both passengers on deck ten filed grievances with corporate and are threatening to report the thefts to the authorities when we dock in Miami."

"Proving a crime of stolen cash will be tough," Millie said.

"Yes, and I've already pointed that out to them. In the meantime, at least for tonight, Gusti will remain in the holding cell. I explained the latest development and assured him it was for his own good."

"Have you tried the compensation route...perhaps offering the passengers a future free cruise or onboard credits?"

"Yes on both. One of them is considering the future cruise and the other, the first guy to report a theft, is refusing both. He's also threatening to hire an attorney and contact local media outlets, insisting Majestic Cruise Lines is unsafe and we operate dangerous ships."

"Oh brother. I'm sorry to hear that," Millie said. "Andy mentioned a guest up on the lido deck is claiming their belongings were removed from a lounge chair, turned in to the ship's crew and now certain items are missing."

"Yes. It happened early this afternoon. We both know this is a common complaint on board the ship," Patterson pointed out. "Donovan issued the guest a generous onboard credit to use in the ship's shops to replace missing items."

Millie and Patterson chatted for a few more minutes, with Millie throwing out theories perhaps the passengers on deck ten were related and reported the thefts as a way to squeeze something out of the cruise line.

"I considered that angle as well. We're looking into a possible connection between the two parties."

Patterson tapped the tip of his nose. "Looks like you got some sun today."

"I did...in between the downpours. Nic and I toured the island on Segways."

"Segways? I like your sense of adventure, Millie. Sky high obstacle courses, zip lining, dune buggies and now Segways."

"None of those were by choice, at least not *my* choice." Millie lifted her fingers for an air quote. "Choice being the key phrase. Nic surprised me - again. I almost died."

Patterson laughed. "C'mon Millie."

"I'm serious. I lost control of the Segway and almost crashed into the curb. I could've cracked my skull wide open," she said dramatically.

"I would think wearing a helmet would be mandatory."

"It was, but that's beside the point," Millie muttered. "Anyhoo, Nic won't be pulling that stunt again anytime soon."

"So you hated the Segway?"

"No. The tour was interesting. We learned a lot about St. Kitts, but I could've done the same from the comfort and safety of a tour bus." Millie took a step back and reached for the doorknob. "I better get out of your hair. Thanks for the update on Gusti."

Millie exited Patterson's office. She slowed as she passed the holding cell, offering up a silent prayer for Gusti and then headed upstairs to the gift shop.

She replayed her conversation with Patterson. There was something in the way he described the lido deck theft, which caused Millie's radar to kick into high alert.

Patterson mentioned that Donovan had issued the passenger whose beach bag and belongings were stolen on the lido deck an onboard credit voucher. There was a chance the passenger stopped by the gift shop to use the voucher and Cat had heard something.

Unfortunately, when she reached the gift shop, she discovered her friend wasn't working.

Millie waited until the store clerk finished ringing up a customer's purchase to approach the counter. "Cat isn't working this afternoon?"

"She just left. I think she was on her way to the crew dining room to grab a bite to eat."

"Thanks." Millie exited the store and headed to the nearest stairwell. When she reached the crew dining room, she caught a glimpse of Cat seated next to another store employee.

Millie slipped inside and approached Cat's table. "Hey, Cat." She nodded to the woman seated across from her friend.

"Hello, Millie. Looks like you got some sun today." Cat patted the empty chair next to her. "Have a seat."

"Nic surprised me with a Segway excursion."

"Segways sound fun," Cat said.

"And dangerous." Millie eased onto the chair. "Don't even get me started."

Cat chuckled. "Other than a little too much sun, you don't look any worse for the wear."

The woman seated across from Cat pushed her chair back. "I better head back upstairs. I'm sure the gift shop is busy now that all of the guests are back on board the ship."

"I'll be up there shortly," Cat promised.

Millie watched the woman drop off her dirty dishes and exit the dining room before turning her attention to her friend. "Andy told me about the guest who reported items missing from her beach bag up on the lido deck. I stopped to ask Patterson about Gusti, who is still in the holding cell. He mentioned Donovan issued the woman a generous onboard credit voucher to compensate for her loss."

"Let me guess...you're here to see if I know anything about it." Cat dipped her French fry in catsup and took a bite.

"I'm trying to figure out if the theft is somehow tied to the two cabin thefts on deck ten. If my memory serves me, the gift shop manager is supposed to verify the credit voucher for purchases in the store."

"Yep. The woman already stopped by the store to redeem it, right before I left for my break." Cat reached for another fry. "I was surprised Donovan issued a hundred and fifty dollar voucher."

"Is that an unusual amount?" Millie asked.

"Oh yeah." Cat told her friend it was common for Donovan to issue credits to guests who reported thefts in public areas. "The amount was unusual. The most I've ever seen is seventy-five bucks and only because the passenger was a diamond elite guest and he raised a big stink."

"I wonder why Donovan issued such a large credit to the woman." Millie grew silent, and she wondered if Patterson was withholding information about the incident.

"When I saw the amount, I wondered if somehow the cabin thefts and the lido deck thefts might be related, too. My theory is Patterson wants the thefts to go away...big time."

"Meaning Patterson and Donovan are hoping the passenger on the lido deck won't pursue filing a complaint," Millie guessed.

"Exactly. I knew it was a theft incident as soon as I saw the voucher. Donovan is the only person authorized to issue those types of vouchers for theft of personal belongings. The high dollar amount was the next clue. Again, it's the first time I've ever seen Donovan issue a credit for this much money."

"Too bad you hadn't thought to ask the person about the theft," Millie said.

"I did." Cat nodded. "Something she said struck me as odd."

Chapter 14

"The woman, Valerie, told me she set her beach bag, a book and a towel on a chair on the upper deck, the one overlooking the pool. She ran inside to grab a bite to eat, and when she got back her stuff was gone, everything except for the beach towel."

Cat explained the woman was furious because there were plenty of empty chairs nearby. "She thinks someone watched her and waited for her to leave. "They stole fifty bucks, a pair of expensive earrings and her iPad."

"Patterson said the bag was turned in to the ship's crew."

"What's interesting is the woman claims the bag was turned in at the tiki bar in the back, not near the main pool, where the woman claims she left the bag and her other belongings."

"That's odd." Millie rubbed her chin. "Why would the thief bother turning the bag in? Why not take what you want and leave it on the chair or toss it in the trashcan? I wonder if the woman's cabin is also on deck ten."

"You know what." Cat snapped her fingers. "I was going to check it out after she left, but forgot. My grumbling stomach distracted me. I'm on my way back to work after I finish eating if you want to head up there with me."

"Yes, that would be perfect."

The conversation shifted to other subjects, and Millie asked Cat if she and Doctor Gundervan were able to patch things up between them after a recent string of spats.

"No. He invited me to dinner a few days ago, but I already made other plans."

"Playing hard to get?" Millie smiled.

Cat's face turned red.

"Ah...you are."

"Not so much playing hard to get. I'm still a little ticked off at him for accusing me of being jealous because of his relationship with Nurse Quaid."

"Speaking of Nurse Quaid, have you met the ship's new nurse?" Millie heard Rachel Quaid's replacement had arrived, but she hadn't met the man yet.

"Yes. His name is Gavin Framm. My guess is he's in his thirties. Nice looking guy, real clean cut and kind of quiet." Cat wiped her mouth and dropped the napkin on top of her empty plate. "You ready to head upstairs to see if we can find out where Valerie's cabin is located?"

"I thought you'd never ask."

The women traipsed out of the dining room. The ship's stores were several flights up, and Cat stopped halfway to catch her breath. "Remind me again, why you won't take the elevators," she gasped.

171

"Because I'm claustrophobic, the elevators aren't any faster than taking the stairs and it's good exercise."

"If you say so." Cat pressed a hand to her flushed cheek. "Let's keep going before I change my mind."

The *Ocean Treasures* gift shop was packed. Cat and Millie wove their way past several displays, dodging shoppers on their way to the cash registers in the back.

Cat swiped her access card and entered her pin code. When the screen popped up, she entered another code to access the onboard system.

"How will you be able to find her?" Millie asked.

"It's simple. We're required to enter the vouchers in a separate screen. I have to verify the voucher number and attach it to the guest's cabin."

"I never knew that," Millie said.

"Corporate is picky about comps and vouchers. Donovan sends detailed reports to them each week, listing the reason for the comp, the purchases the passenger made and the guest's information."

"Hmm." Millie leaned in. "I suppose the information is useful in the event the passenger decides to file a claim or complaint against the cruise line. We would have some sort of record of what transpired."

"Exactly." Cat slipped her reading glasses on and tapped the keys. "Her full name is Valerie Yost. She's in cabin ninety-two zero nine."

"Cabin ninety-two zero nine." Millie pinched her chin thoughtfully. "The other thefts were on deck ten."

"But her cabin wasn't broken into," Cat pointed out.

"True. I was trying to figure out if there was a link between the cabins and the thefts. There doesn't appear to be." Millie circled the counter. "I wish you could talk to her again."

"She'll be back," Cat predicted. "She didn't use all of her credits. She still has about fifty bucks left to spend. I can keep an eye out for her; try to glean a little more information when she comes back in."

"That would be great," Millie said. "You're the best."

"Maybe we can figure out what's going on and help Gusti. I know what it feels like to be wrongly accused." Cat logged out of the computer system. "I better get back to work. Our mega blowout inch of gold sale starts soon, and this place is going to be a madhouse."

"Which is my cue to hightail it out of here before the masses arrive and my claustrophobia kicks into high gear."

With some time to kill before her shift started and since the galley was close by, Millie decided to pick Annette's brain about the string of thefts.

The dinner rush hadn't begun and it was Annette's downtime, a time she used to tinker with new recipes.

She found her friend standing at the counter, surrounded by a mixing bowl and an array of ingredients.

Amit stood across from her with another mixing bowl, contemplating the bowl's contents.

Millie waved her arms to get his attention. "Hey, Amit."

"Miss Millie." Amit shifted his gaze. "You got some sun. The captain surprised you with a beach day?"

"Not quite. We rode Segways."

"Segways?" Annette waited for Millie to join them. "You know how to ride a Segway?"

"I do now, after a near spill and potentially catastrophic injury."

Annette laughed. "It sounds like there's more to the story."

"There is. I'll tell you another time." Millie pointed to her friend's mixing bowl. "What are you making?"

"We're working on Andy's reindeer theme," Annette said. "Amit is whipping up a reindeer cheese ball, and I'm testing out a chocolate reindeer for the kid's Christmas party with Santa. According to Andy, Santa's first visit is this Sunday."

"Chocolate reindeer?" Millie eased in next to Annette. "I'm intrigued."

Annette explained the sweet treat was a combination of crushed Oreo cookies, mixed with cream cheese and vanilla. "After I form the heads, I stick them in the refrigerator for a few minutes to harden. Check it out. I have a sample batch ready to go."

She darted over to the fridge and returned carrying a tray of round, black balls. "I just finished melting the chocolate."

Annette balanced one of the balls on a clean fork and then dipped it in the bowl of melted chocolate. After dipping it in chocolate, she gingerly rolled it onto a sheet of wax paper. "The trick is to add the antlers before the chocolate cools."

Millie watched her break a pretzel and wiggle a broken piece into each side of the reindeer's chocolate head. "Next, we add the eyes and nose and Voila! You have an adorable yet totally edible reindeer."

"How clever." Millie clapped her hands. "My grandchildren would love these. I wonder if we could add this to the children's Christmas activities."

"Kids fiddling with a mixing bowl filled with hot, melted chocolate?" Annette shook her head.

"I hadn't thought of that. Maybe we'll stick to frosting cookies." Millie turned to Amit. "What are you working on again?"

"A reindeer cheeseball, one of several new items for the Christmas tea party Annette is adding next week."

"A Christmas tea party sounds intriguing."

"The reindeer cheeseball is for Andy's reindeer theme. The rest are classic tea party items, but with a holiday twist." Annette led Millie to a tiered tray in the corner, loaded with tasty treats. "I'm tinkering with a modified holiday fruitcake, filled with oranges, coconut, dates, raisins and nuts."

"They're shaped like mini Christmas trees," Millie said. "What a great idea."

"Check out my egg and cress tea sandwiches. I dug out my star-shaped cookie cutters to cut pieces of white and wheat bread. The mixture of breads gives the sandwiches a different texture and flavor."

"How creative." Millie noticed a large crockpot near the back. "What's in there?"

"This...this is my favorite." Annette lifted the lid, and a burst of cinnamon and spices filled the air. "It's my special spiced apple cider. Doesn't it smell heavenly?"

"It does. I don't suppose you need a taste tester," Millie hinted.

"I can always use another opinion." Annette plucked a ladle from the utensil drawer. She scooped out a generous serving and ladled it into a nearby teacup before handing it to Millie. "We'll be serving it during the Christmas tree trimming event this afternoon. That and a batch of old-fashioned Christmas cookies shaped like reindeer, of course."

"Of course. Thank you." Millie lifted the cup, savoring the aroma before taking a tentative sip. "This is delicious. It will be perfect for the tree decorating festivities."

"I thought so, too." Annette nodded approvingly.

"I don't mind sampling the cheeseball either." Millie patted her stomach. "I love a good cheese ball."

"You're in luck, Miss Millie. I have one chilling." Amit hurried to the fridge. He returned with a large cheese ball, covered in walnuts and sporting the same pretzel antlers as the children's chocolate reindeer.

He rummaged around inside the cabinet and pulled out a box of snack crackers. "You must try it with crackers."

"I can't wait." Millie grabbed a knife from the drawer and sawed off a large chunk.

Amit handed her a cracker, and she eased the slab of cheese on top before taking a big bite. The salty ham and bacon mingled with a hint of tart made her taste buds tingle. "It's salty and tart."

"We used bacon bits and ham. The tart is a dash of Worcestershire sauce," Annette explained.

"Delicious." Millie sliced off another generous chunk. "I need to try a little more, just to be sure." She gobbled the second piece and set the knife on the counter. "These are all hands down winners."

"So what brings you to my neck of the woods?" Annette asked.

"Another theft." Millie briefly told Annette and Amit about the incident on the lido deck.

"How would a serial thief know to snatch up a specific bag?" Amit asked.

"That's a good question. Why pick that specific person and/or a specific bag?"

Annette tapped the side of her forehead. "Motive and opportunity."

"You're right. Motive would be stealing something of value and opportunity would be the person walked away, leaving the belongings wide open for someone with sticky fingers to come along and take it."

"Or maybe they watched the woman," Amit said. "Maybe they knew what was inside the beach bag, they waited until she left and then they stole it."

"True. I mean, it makes sense." There was still something nagging in the back of Millie's mind…something wasn't adding up. "All I know is there have been three thefts…two on deck ten and one on the lido deck."

"I bet she won't leave her stuff on the deck chairs again," Annette predicted. "They're not supposed to save deck chairs anyways."

"You said it, sister," Millie said. "Oh…and Andy said someone took off with one of the small reindeer we placed in the *Sprinkles* window display."

"Now that's a theft that needs to be investigated," Annette joked.

"Right?" Millie lifted her eyes skyward. "This reindeer theme has gone right to Andy's head."

Millie's radio began to squawk. It was Andy.

"Millie, do you copy?"

"His ears must be burning." Millie unclipped her radio and pressed the button.

"Go ahead, Andy."

"We have a problem. I need for you to meet me in the *Marseille Lounge* right away."

Chapter 15

Millie thanked her friends for the yummy treats before heading to the lounge. When she arrived, she found Dave Patterson, Oscar and Andy all gathered around the small stage.

"What's going on?"

"This." Patterson pointed at the stage floor and Millie's name; painted in bright red letters. There appeared to be a large drop of blood next to her name.

"What in the world?" Millie tentatively touched the letters. "Someone vandalized the stage and wrote my name? Who would do such a crazy thing?"

"This woman." Patterson handed Millie his cell phone. "We caught her on surveillance camera. It happened late last night after the lounge closed."

Millie's eyes squinted as she silently studied the short video. "It's Tracy what's-her-name."

"Tracy Robinson," Patterson said. "You know her?"

"She's been stalking me ever since the *Killer Karaoke* incident, when I ended the karaoke early and she didn't get to sing. She's been following me around the ship harassing me."

Millie continued. "I didn't want to make a big deal out of it. I've been swapping events with other staff members when she shows up. I haven't heard a peep out of her since the ornament decorating run-in and I hoped she'd given up."

She ran a light hand over the letters. "This paint looks like the same acrylic paint we use for the ornament decorating. She must've pocketed a jar and a paintbrush, snuck in here and wrote my name."

"She hasn't given up. In fact, it appears she upped her level of harassment," Patterson said. "I

185

don't understand why missing out on singing karaoke would set her off, to make her want to harass you, not to mention vandalize our ship."

"I don't get it either," Millie confessed. "I tried talking to her. I even offered to let her be the first in line for the next round of karaoke, but she refused and appears determined to make my life miserable. She's doing an excellent job, I might add."

"We're going to get to the bottom of this." Patterson reached for his radio. "Donovan has access to all of the passenger's information. We'll see if he has time to let us take a closer look at Ms. Robinson's profile."

They were in luck, and Donovan was in his office. Patterson and Oscar led the way inside. Millie was sandwiched in between, and Andy brought up the rear.

"I didn't know we were having a party," Donovan kidded.

"I wish it was a party," Millie muttered. "We're here to investigate a passenger."

"Tracy Robinson," Patterson said. "We caught her on camera, vandalizing the *Marseille Lounge* late last night. She painted Millie's name on the stage."

Donovan shifted in his chair, a look of concern on his face. "Has she given a reason for vandalizing the lounge?"

"We haven't talked to her yet. We were hoping you could tell us a little more about her before Patterson confronts her," Andy said.

"Why Millie's name?" Donovan asked.

"I cut the *Killer Karaoke* set short the other day. She was next in line to sing, and she got ticked off," Millie said.

"It seems…a little unbalanced to paint your name on ship property because she couldn't sing karaoke."

"She also heckled me during the *Heart and Homes* show, disrupted the ornament decorating activity and now this," Millie said miserably. "She'll probably try to push me overboard next."

"That's not funny," Andy said sternly. "We're going to get to the bottom of this."

"Let me see what I have on her." Donovan turned his attention to his computer screen. "Interesting."

"What?" Millie inched forward. "What did you find?"

Donovan shot Millie a quick glance. "Are you sure you don't know Ms. Robinson?"

"Positive. I've never met her before in my life."

"She lives in Grand Rapids, Michigan."

"No kidding. Tracy Robinson." Millie repeated her name. "Tracy Robinson. No. I have no idea who she is."

"What else do you know?" Patterson asked.

"She's in her late fifties. Government issued passport. This is her first cruise on Majestic Cruise Lines. She listed Gail Robinson as her emergency contact."

"Did you leave any enemies behind in Michigan?" Andy joked.

"Other than my ex-husband, Roger? I don't think so."

"What about your children? Is it possible they might recognize the name?" Oscar asked.

"Could be. Let me give Beth and Blake a call." Millie excused herself and stepped out of the office. She headed to a quiet corner, near the window and pulled her cell phone from her pocket. She connected to the ship's Wi-Fi to get the call to go through.

Beth didn't answer. Millie left a brief message asking her daughter to call her back right away, explaining she had a quick question. While she waited, she decided to try Blake's cell phone.

"Hi, Mom. Aren't you working?"

"Yes. I'm on the ship. We're heading to Grand Turk. I have a quick question."

"Sure."

"Does the name Tracy Robinson ring a bell?"

"Tracy Robinson." There was a long pause before Blake spoke. "No. The name doesn't sound familiar. Why?"

"Because there's a Tracy Robinson on board the Siren of the Seas and she's stalking me."

"Stalking you? How?"

"She's following me to my events and harassing me. Early this morning, she painted my name on one of the lounge stages." Millie left off the part about the splotch of blood.

"You should report her to security." Blake sounded alarmed.

"Security is working on it now. That's how I found out she's from the Grand Rapids area. I wondered if you knew her."

"I wish I could help. Did you check with Beth?"

"I left her a message." Millie's phone beeped, and she glanced at the screen. "Beth is calling in."

"Be careful," Blake said.

"I will." Millie told her son she loved him before disconnecting and answering Beth's call. "Hello, Beth."

"Hey, Mom. You don't have to keep calling to check on me and the kids. We're fine."

"That's not why I'm calling," Millie said. "I was wondering if the name Tracy Robinson rings a bell."

"Tracy...Robinson. Gosh. It sounds familiar." Beth grew quiet. "I...do you think she may have hired dad to investigate, maybe he worked on something for her?"

"I don't know. Is there any way you can find out?"

"Sure. Something makes me think I've heard Dad mention the name. I can call him to ask and then call you back."

"I have to head back to a meeting." Millie consulted her watch. "It's six now. I'm hosting an event soon. Why don't I call you at seven-thirty after it ends?"

"Perfect. I'll see what I can find out."

Millie thanked her daughter before hanging up and returned to Donovan's office. All eyes were on her as she stepped back inside the room. "My daughter, Beth, thinks the name sounds familiar. She's going to do some checking around. I told her I would call her back at seven-thirty to see if she was able to come up with anything."

"I'll hold off on talking to Ms. Robinson until we hear if there's some sort of connection between her and you." Patterson stood - his signal the meeting was over.

Millie was the last to leave, and Donovan motioned her to stay behind. "Please be careful Millie. At the very least, the passenger appears to be somewhat unstable."

She promised Donovan she would, and then exited the office.

It was time for her to start *Worldwide Trivia,* a trivia game she'd found online and was lucky enough to tie into the Caribbean cruise ports.

The trivia ended, and Millie headed to a quiet corner to call Beth back. Unfortunately, her daughter hadn't been able to reach her father.

"I'll try calling again after bingo ends around nine-thirty," Millie said. "Is that too late? I know your day was stressful to say the least, and I'm sure you want to head to bed early."

"Nine-thirty is fine," Beth assured her. "Besides, Dad was going to check on us tonight. The timing is perfect. He usually calls around nine."

Millie ended the call and joined Felix, her co-host, on the theater's stage. During setup, she kept one eye on the passengers who began to straggle in, certain at any moment Tracy would appear.

The first round of bingo began, with the jackpot at a hundred and fifty dollars. It was a quick game with a single winner. Felix and Millie moved on to four corners bingo with a winning jackpot of a hundred and seventy-five dollars.

More players began filing in, and Millie suspected it was because the final round of bingo featured the *Cruise or Cash* bingo game. The game's winner was given the option of choosing between a suite cruise or a cash prize of two thousand dollars.

The room filled and Felix and Millie began working the crowd, selling stacks of bingo cards as if they were going out of style.

Millie extended the cutoff for as long as she dared before returning to the center of the stage and turning the microphone on. "Thank you for joining us for the most popular bingo game of the cruise…our *Cruise or Cash* bingo. This is your chance to win either a seven-day suite cruise or two thousand dollars in cash."

There were several whoops of excitement from the audience, and the chatter grew louder. "For this game, our fun-filled final round, we're going to play full house bingo."

A collective groan rang out, and Millie lifted her hand. "C'mon folks. This is a wonderful prize, and someone WILL win."

Millie was new to full house bingo before joining the Siren of the Seas. The game required the winner to fill in every single space on a bingo card, except for the free space.

Felix flipped the switch on the bingo ball machine, and Millie began to call. The game lasted longer than anticipated. She started to sweat it out, concerned the bingo would spill over into the time passengers started arriving for the *Waves of Wonder* show.

"I got it!" a young woman shrieked. "I mean...Bingo!" She sprang from her seat and began jumping up and down.

"C'mon down." Millie waved the woman to the stage where Felix checked her card to verify a win.

"We have a winner," Millie announced.

"Oh my gosh." The woman clapped her hands. "I've never won before. What did I win?"

The crowd began to laugh.

Millie placed a light arm around her shoulder. "Honey, you won the grand prize. It's your pick. You either get a seven-day cruise for two on board the Siren of the Seas or any other Majestic Cruise Line ship and in a suite no less...or two thousand dollars cash."

The woman's arms began to tremble. Millie, concerned she might faint, tightened her grip. "What's your name?"

"Julia. Julia Koster."

"Are you here with family, Julia?"

"No. I'm here with my best friend, Cristina...Cris."

"Well, lucky you and Cris. Perhaps you can buy her a latte up in the specialty coffee shop when this is over."

"Oh. I'll definitely do that." Julia nodded enthusiastically.

"So what are you going to choose, Julia? Would you like the seven-day suite cruise or the two thousand dollars cash?" Millie asked.

Julia peered into the audience and began signaling with her hands. She turned to Millie. "I'm going to take the cash."

The crowd cheered enthusiastically, a popular choice with previous *Cruise or Cash* winners.

"Congratulations." Millie kept close to the ecstatic winner and turned to the crowd. "Next up is our spectacular *Waves of Wonder* show. If you haven't seen it before ladies and gentlemen, it's fantastic." Millie turned the mike off and led Julia down the side steps.

"Julia." A woman jogged down the center aisle and joined them. "I can't believe you won."

"I know." Julia hugged the woman. "I thought I was going to pass out."

"For a minute, I thought so, too," Millie teased. "We'll need to get your cabin number and verify your identification at guest services where you can collect your cash."

It was a short walk from the theater to the guest services desk. Julia promptly produced her picture identification and waited for the guest services clerk to count out the cash.

Julia folded the stack of bills in half and shoved them in her front pocket.

"You may want to lock the loot in your safe." Millie thought of the recent string of thefts.

"I will," Julia promised.

Millie waited until Julia and her friend departed before heading upstairs to grab a light snack, remembering Nic had planned a romantic dinner for two later in the evening.

She decided on a slice of pizza and small side salad before heading to an empty table. While she ate, she thought about her stalker, Tracy.

There was obviously some sort of connection between Millie and Tracy, but what? The fact the woman's name sounded familiar to Beth and she thought her father, Millie's ex, might have mentioned the name was a clue.

Hopefully, Beth would be able to make a connection.

Millie finished her food before heading to the piano bar to check on the early round of sing-alongs.

Her next stop was *Killer Karaoke* to make sure things were running smoothly. She had enough time to peek in on the comedy show before making her way to a secluded spot to call Beth.

At nine-thirty on the dot, Millie dialed her daughter's cell phone number.

A breathless Beth answered. "I found out who Tracy Robinson is. You're never going to believe this."

Chapter 16

"Who is she?" A queasy feeling settled in the pit of Millie's stomach, and she was certain she wasn't going to like her daughter's answer.

"She is...was...Delilah Osborne's best friend, Tracy Robinson."

Millie's scalp tingled. "Why would she come on this ship and stalk me?"

"Revenge. Dad said after Delilah died, she started acting crazy, talking about how you were responsible for Delilah's death and how she was going to make you pay for murdering her friend."

"Th-that's absurd," Millie sputtered. "I had nothing to do with Delilah's death."

"The woman is unstable."

"That's an understatement."

"Dad was shocked she was on board your ship. He had no idea she planned to book a cruise and follow through with her threats. It is close to the anniversary of Delilah's death."

"You're right." Millie's pulse quickened. "Delilah died almost a year ago."

"Yep. Promise me you'll tell your security people right now. You're not safe," Beth said.

"As soon as I hang up, I'll track down our head of security." Millie assured her daughter she would be careful and thanked her for the information before disconnecting the call.

Millie strode to the stairs and took them two at a time. When she reached Patterson's office, she was relieved to find the lights were on and he was inside.

Patterson gave her a quick glance and then did a double take. "You look like you're ready to explode. Let me guess...you found a connection to Tracy Robinson."

"Do you remember last year, when my ex-husband brought his fiancée, Delilah Osborne, on the ship, insisting Nic...Captain Armati marry them, and then Delilah mysteriously died?"

"And your ex accused you of murdering the woman, but we found out differently." Patterson clasped his hands. "How could I forget?"

"Well, Tracy Robinson is - was Delilah's best friend. She told my ex she's going to make me pay for killing Delilah. This is near the anniversary of her death, and she's determined to...gosh, I don't even know. At the very least, she'll probably try to have me fired."

Patterson rubbed his chin. "I'll know more once I have a chance to chat with her."

"What about giving me a gun?"

"You want me to give you a gun?"

"I'm kidding." Millie briefly closed her eyes.

"You do tend to attract the crazies."

Her eyes flew open. "Thanks."

"You're welcome. Where is that slick flashlight/Taser Andy gave you right after you started working on the ship?"

"It's in my closet. The batteries are dead."

"Take it out of the closet, put some new batteries in it and start carrying it at all times until the ship docks on Saturday and Ms. Robinson disembarks."

Patterson offered Millie a few more suggestions on staying safe for the next two days. "Do you want me to talk to Andy, to see if he can pull you off your shifts until the ship arrives back in Miami?"

"No." Millie firmly shook her head. "If she forces me into hiding, she wins."

"But at least you're still alive," Patterson pointed out.

"Do you really think she'll try to take me out?"

"I have no idea. Her actions scream emotional instability. If she believes you played a part in her best friend's death, it's hard to say what she'll do." Patterson assured her he would increase security around the ship before reminding Millie to dig her flashlight/Taser from the closet and carry it with her.

Millie trudged back to the apartment where Nic was already waiting. She kicked her shoes off and wandered into the dining room.

"You look like you lost your best friend," Nic said.

"No. I'm being stalked by Delilah Osborne's best friend. She's on the ship to pay me back on the anniversary of Delilah's death."

"Delilah Osborne." Nic frowned. "The name sounds familiar."

"It was my ex-husband's fiancée...the one who was on board the ship and died. Her best friend blames me, and since this is the anniversary of her death, it's payback time."

"That's crazy," Nic said. "Surely, she can't be serious. What person would book a cruise, get on the ship and then harass the assistant cruise director when the real killer was caught and confessed?"

"A person with emotional issues." Millie absentmindedly picked Scout up. "I already talked to Patterson. Since the woman hasn't technically threatened me, only harassed me and painted my name on one of the lounge stages, he's reluctant to detain her."

"She painted your name?" Nic roared.

"Painted it in bright, blood-red letters. Next to it was what looked like a large splotch of dripping blood."

"That does it." Nic marched to the kitchen and snatched his radio off the counter. "I want Patterson to pick this woman up and detain her until we dock in Miami."

"Other than vandalizing a stage, she hasn't done anything. She hasn't physically threatened me," Millie argued.

"We can't stand by and wait to see what she does next." Nic squared his shoulders. "Andy needs to take you off duty. You can spend the next couple of days here in the apartment or on the bridge with me."

"No." Millie stubbornly shook her head. "Then she wins."

"We're talking about an extremely unstable individual," Nic said.

"Agreed. I'm going to take Patterson's advice, dig out my Taser and keep it handy. If or when she tries something, she'll get the shock of her life and then Patterson can lock her up."

It took several minutes for Millie to calm her husband and convince him she would be okay.

"Let's compromise. You can keep working if you agree to buddy up with someone for the next two days."

Millie tilted her head. "It...might work. I could see if Danielle. No." She quickly dismissed the idea.

"I can't short staff the entertainment department. Let me think."

"While you think of a partner, I'll start setting the table."

Millie was so distracted over Tracy's identity that the server's cart, the white linen tablecloth draped over the dining room table and the soft candlelight hadn't registered yet.

"How romantic." Millie smiled softly. "You did all of this for me?"

"Of course. I would do that and more." Nic arranged the forks on top of the dinner napkins and made his way to his wife's side. He drew her into his arms. "You're my everything, Millie. You make me laugh. You drive me crazy. You keep me on my toes."

"I do?"

"Of course." Nic caressed his wife's cheek before gently pulling her close and kissing her tenderly.

Millie closed her eyes. A warm flush swept through her as she abandoned herself to the man she loved, the man she'd found after years of unhappiness, the man she vowed to grow old with.

Her breath caught in her throat as the kiss deepened.

Finally, Nic pulled back, his breath ragged. "We may have to forget about dinner."

"Dinner?" Millie's eyelids drooped. "We have plenty of time to eat...later."

"I couldn't agree more." Nic blew out the candles and reached for his wife's hand before leading her up the stairs.

*****

While eating dinner, Nic brought up the subject of Millie teaming up with another crewmember again. "You only have the rest of today and tomorrow."

"I know. I've been wracking my brain, trying to come up with the perfect person. No one comes to mind. Most of the people I feel comfortable asking are part of the entertainment staff and already have their set schedules."

"So you need someone with flexibility."

"Where is my buddy Nadia when I need her?" Millie joked.

"Nadia would be the perfect person. Too bad she's in St. Martin." Nic sipped his coffee, eyeing his wife over the rim. "What about the employee who was a former golf pro? Isis something?"

"Isla?" Millie chewed the corner of her lip. "I hadn't thought about her. She's a little rough around the edges."

"She's a scrapper, which is exactly what you need," Nic said.

"But I don't know Isla that well."

"Do you have a better suggestion?"

"No." Millie knew she was fighting a losing battle. "Fine. Isla it is, but only if Andy can spare her."

"He'll spare her." Nic waited until they finished their meal and the room service staff collected the dirty dishes to call Andy.

It was a brief conversation, and when Nic hung up, he smiled triumphantly. "You're to meet Andy and Isla in his office at seven tomorrow morning. You'll work together until the ship docks in Miami on Saturday."

"That was easy," Millie said.

"Now I won't have to worry about you and your safety."

The couple wandered onto the balcony to enjoy the cool evening air and chatted about the upcoming day.

Finally, Millie couldn't keep her eyes open. "I'm exhausted."

"Me, too." Nic coaxed Scout inside, and the trio headed up the stairs. It didn't take long for Millie to conk out. She slept through the night and woke with a start when the alarm sounded.

Despite the restful sleep, she was still groggy and headed downstairs to start a pot of coffee.

Nic joined her a short time later. He filled his thermos and secured the lid before kissing his wife tenderly. "Remember your promise?"

"Yes. Isla is my pal, my partner, my buddy for the entire day."

"For your own safety. You have your Taser?"

"I'll dig it out of the closet as soon as I get dressed," Millie promised. "I won't even have to use the Taser. All I'll have to do is give someone a good whack on the side of the head and knock them out cold."

"Hopefully, it won't be necessary." Nic gave his wife a hug and then headed out of the apartment.

Millie wasn't far behind her husband. After dressing, she let Scout onto the balcony for one final break before making her way to Andy's office.

She could hear muffled voices coming from within. "Hello?" Millie stuck her head inside the doorway where Andy and Isla stood talking.

"Millie. You're right on time," Andy said. "Isla is excited to learn a little more about the ins and outs of being an assistant cruise director."

"Thank you for agreeing to help on such short notice." Millie stepped into the office.

"I filled Isla in on the reason she'll be partnering with you, as well as shown her a picture of Ms. Robinson."

"Thanks, Andy. If we hurry, Isla and I will have time to grab a quick bite to eat up on the lido deck before beginning our sunrise stride."

"Before you take off, I have one more thing to tell you."

"What's that?"

"There was another theft last night."

Chapter 17

Millie said the first thing that popped into her head. "Is Gusti still in the holding cell?"

"Patterson released him early this morning. Kimel Pang moved Gusti to another deck. He's working on deck two today."

"That's great news," Millie said. "Not about the theft. About Gusti returning to work. What happened?"

"Patterson called me right before I turned in last night. He said the woman who won the grand prize bingo yesterday reported someone broke into her cabin and stole money from her cabin safe."

"Julia? You're kidding? I hosted that bingo game. After she won, I escorted her and her friend to guest services to sign some papers and collect the cash."

"She collected it all right and then someone broke into her cabin and stole it."

"How awful."

"Patterson is ready to rip his hair out."

"No kidding. How many does that make, if you include the passenger who claimed someone took items from their beach bag on the lido deck?"

"We're up to four. Two on deck ten, the lido deck beach bag theft and now the bingo burglary. I'm sure Patterson will want to question you about Julia's winnings and your conversation with her." Andy followed Millie and Isla to the door. "Be careful out there today."

As if on cue, Patterson radioed Millie before Isla and she made it to the theater's exit.

"I guess our breakfast will have to wait for a few more minutes," Millie apologized.

"I'm not much of an early breakfast person. When Andy asked me if I wanted to buddy up with you, I jumped at the chance to work with the infamous shipboard sleuth, Millie." Isla rubbed her hands together. "I didn't realize I would be part of an investigation this quickly."

"It's not technically my investigation," Millie said. "Patterson doesn't like it when I butt into his business, although depending on what he wants to discuss, that might change."

Millie gave Patterson's office door a warning knock and then pushed it open. He didn't appear surprised to see Isla, and she suspected Andy mentioned he'd found someone to team up with her.

"Thanks for stopping by. I assume Andy mentioned there was another theft last night."

"Yes. He said it involved yesterday's bingo jackpot winner, Julia Koster. I hosted the winning bingo game and then accompanied her to guest services to show her ID and collect her cash," Millie said.

"I wanted to get your take on her personally. Did she say anything which struck you as odd, maybe make an offhand joke she needed the money or what she planned to do with the cash?" Patterson asked.

"No. She was obviously thrilled. I told her to make sure to take the cash back to her cabin and lock it up in the safe. I guess she didn't take my advice."

Patterson gave Millie a funny look.

"She claims she locked the money in the safe and it was stolen?" Millie gasped. "How can that be?"

"I hoped the beach bag theft was unrelated to the first two thefts on deck ten. It appears we have a serial thief on board the ship."

"I didn't think to ask Julia where her cabin was located. Is it on deck ten?"

"No. She and her friend are in an interior cabin on deck one." Patterson's jaw tightened. "It's easy to see how Julia might be the target of a thief. She won the bingo jackpot. All it would take is for someone to follow her back to her cabin, wait for her to leave and then break in."

"But the keycards," Millie said. "I don't understand how this keeps happening. Unless it's an employee using their keycard to access the cabin, how would they get in, let alone break into a guest's safe?"

"Although most people wouldn't know this, there is a way to get into the cabin without being detected and without having the cabin's keycard," Patterson said.

"You think whoever is stealing from the passengers knows how to break into passenger cabins?"

"I'm afraid so. One of my guys is in the process of checking the Cruise Line Incident Reports to see if there's a recent pattern of thefts on board other cruise lines. I checked with corporate, and we're the first to report a string of suspicious thefts."

Millie shifted her feet. "What is the Cruise Line Incident Reports?"

Patterson explained it was a government website. "It's a database, a place for cruise ships to report crimes." He rattled off the list including missing U.S. Nationals, sexual assaults, deaths, tampering with a vessel and, of course, thefts.

"You should report Tracy Robinson for tampering with a vessel," Millie joked.

Patterson shook his head.

"I was joking. Getting back to our conundrum. There has to be a common thread, someone who knows these passengers have money."

Isla, who had been silent during Patterson and Millie's conversation, spoke. "Most people carry at least some cash on board the ship, for purchases in ports, for taxis and tips or the casino."

"True." Millie patted her pockets. "Do you mind if I borrow a pen and some paper?"

Patterson eyed her warily before handing her a yellow pad. "Tell me you're not going to start nosing around in the thefts."

"I'm not going to nose around in the thefts." Millie held out her hand. "Pen please."

Patterson reluctantly handed her a pen.

Millie perched on the edge of a chair and began jotting some notes. "So we have four reported thefts."

"I thought you said you weren't going to stick your nose in my business."

"No." Millie shook her head. "You said, 'Tell me you're not going to start nosing around in the thefts', so I did."

She scribbled as she talked. "The first theft was on deck ten, in Gusti's section. The passenger claims he had cash in his safe and someone stole it."

Millie rattled off the second theft, also on deck ten. "That's when you brought Gusti to the holding cell, but now it appears the thefts on the same deck were merely coincidental."

"The third theft was opportunity where the passenger left valuable items on a deck chair. The items were stolen and the beach bag, minus the valuables, was turned in to the deck staff."

"Correct. We've checked the deck cameras and aren't able to pinpoint the person who turned in the items," Patterson acknowledged. "Now, we have Ms. Koster's bingo winnings theft, but on deck one."

"Is it possible a crewmember, maybe even someone who works in security, is the thief?" Millie asked. "It would have to be someone with access to the cabins, who wouldn't appear suspicious. They would have to find a way to work around the keycard monitoring system."

"And figure out how to crack the code on the safes," Isla added.

Millie tapped the pen on top of the pad of paper. "If we can figure out how all of these link together, we can start closing in on the culprit."

"There is no 'we,' Millie. You aren't a part of this investigation." Patterson gave her a pointed stare. "You have enough on your plate with your stalker. The last thing you should be worrying about is random thefts."

Millie ripped off the sheet of paper and slid the pen and yellow pad across Patterson's desk. "These are not random. There's a connection." She stopped short of admitting she was going to start her own investigation.

Instead, she simply folded the sheet of paper and tucked it in her front pocket. "I hear you let Gusti out and he's on the job again."

"Yes. He's a happy man," Patterson said.

"I'm sure he is. Good luck on your investigation," Millie said sincerely. "I hope you figure out who is stealing from the passengers before a criminal walks off the ship in less than forty-eight hours with stolen cash and leaving a trail of ruined vacations."

"Don't remind me," Patterson said glumly.

Millie followed Isla out of the office and down the long corridor. The crew mess was a beehive of activity. "I say we hit the lido today and skip the crowds down here."

When they reached the buffet, Millie loaded her plate with a spoonful of scrambled eggs, several slices of bacon, a toasted bagel and an apple. She poured a cup of coffee and then joined Isla at a table for two.

Isla waited for Millie to take her seat and pray over her food. "Do you think one of the crewmembers stole from the passengers?"

"No." Millie took a bite of her apple and chewed thoughtfully. "We haven't had a crew changeover in months. If a crewmember was responsible for the thefts, why would the thief wait until now and why all at once?"

"True," Isla agreed.

"Patterson made an interesting comment. Someone would have to have the experience to work around the keycard system. They would also have to know how to work around the safes' locking mechanisms."

"The internet is a great search tool," Isla said.

"I was thinking the same thing. After we finish our morning shift, we're going to head down to the employee's computers to do a little digging around."

With a plan in place, the women quickly finished their food and began the sunrise stride.

Next up was Millie's first round of trivia. Tracy was nowhere in sight. Millie hoped that since it was a port day, the woman decided to get off the ship in Grand Turk, and she and Isla would have a peaceful, conflict-free day.

Isla easily kept up as they moved from the arts and crafts project to a ping-pong elimination round.

The morning ended with them supervising an art auction.

The art auction attendance was almost non-existent. Millie had heard through the grapevine that there was a chance the cruise line would not renew the art gallery's contract.

Because of the lack of attendance, Millie decided they could scoot out a little early. "Let's head to the computers to start our research."

"Sounds like a plan." Isla hummed as they headed to the stairwell and Millie smiled. Although she preferred working alone, Isla was easygoing, a definite change of pace from Danielle's nonstop go-go personality.

"So what's your background, Isla? I know you're a former golf instructor. Where are you from? What made you want to join the Siren of the Seas?"

"I'm from Florida, home to several championship golf courses. I got bored and on a whim, decided to research working on board a cruise ship."

Isla explained when she told her parents she landed a job interview; they freaked out, but then calmed down, thinking she would never snag the job. "They tried everything they could to get me to turn it down. We struck a deal...I signed up for one contract. If I didn't like it, I would be back in Florida in less than a year."

"And this is your first contract."

"Yep." Isla smiled, the dimple in her cheek deepening. "And it won't be my last. How many people get paid to travel all over the world, not to mention get a free room and food?"

"I agree. I take it you're looking forward to the British Isles itinerary?"

"You bet. I spend my free time researching the ports and things to do. Do you know we're visiting Blarney Castle? The first thing I'm going to do is kiss the Blarney Stone."

Millie laughed. "Better you than me. I don't need a gift for gab."

They reached the employee computer station, and Millie chose a seat near the back, facing out. "I'm paranoid someone might sneak up behind me and spy on me."

"Spoken like a true sleuth." Isla sat next to Millie. "You're going to research entering a cruise ship cabin undetected and also how to break into a cruise ship cabin safe?"

"Or a hotel room safe," Millie clarified. "Why don't you research accessing a cabin undetected while I see what I can find on breaking into a cruise ship cabin safe?"

"Okay."

The women swiped their keycards and began their research.

Millie typed in, "How to break into a cruise ship cabin safe." Nothing came up. She tried, "How to break into a hotel room safe."

"I think I found something." Millie slipped her reading glasses on and clicked on the top result, *The secret master code thieves use to break into hotel room safes.* She skimmed the article and then clicked on the short video.

Millie elbowed her partner. "Isla, you've got to see this."

Chapter 18

Isla scooted closer to Millie. "You found something?"

"Maybe. Check this out." Millie clicked the mouse.

The video showed a man placing a wallet inside a safe, similar to the ones on board the Siren of the Seas. He entered a four-digit code and then tugged on the handle to confirm it was locked.

Next, he entered a wrong code, and an error flashed across the digital display.

Millie turned the volume up. "Check this out."

The camera panned back to the man before focusing on the front of the safe. "What most end users, including hotels and cruise ships, fail to do is reset the administrator password, also known as the default code, after purchasing the safes from the factory."

"Now we're going to put the locking system into super-user mode." He pressed the lock button twice followed by six number nines.

The safe made a faint whirring noise, and the door popped open. "A series of nines, zeroes or ones is the standard default for most digital safes. It could be four nines, all the way up to six nines, depending on the model and manufacturer. My advice is the next time you check into a hotel, check to make sure the safe isn't set at the default. You and your valuables might not be safe, after all."

Isla's mouth fell open. "No kidding. We need to check it out."

"I wonder if Patterson is aware of this."

"He's not in charge of safes, is he?"

"No, but this would fall under safety and security issues." Millie snorted. "Get it? Safe-ty issue?"

Isla rolled her eyes. "Oh, brother."

"Did you find anything?" Millie asked.

"Not yet." Isla turned her attention back to her computer. She grew quiet as she tapped the keys. "I've tried searching different key phrases and so far nothing."

Millie leaned in. "Try master keycard copycats or something along those lines."

Isla typed in the exact phrase. "I think we're onto something." She clicked on a link, *A Hack to Create a Hotel Room Master Key*.

The article explained how a security company figured out a way to reprogram old, expired or discarded keycards to open any door with keycard capabilities.

"Did you read the second paragraph?" Isla whispered.

Millie was just getting to it. Her heart pounded loudly in her chest as she read the next sentence.

"The company was able to modify the keycard, so it wouldn't trip any alerts."

She stared at the screen in disbelief. "That's it. Someone on board this ship has the background or knowledge to not only create a trackless master keycard but has figured out how to open cabin safes."

"Someone with security experience," Isla guessed.

"Exactly." Millie pounded her fist on the desk in frustration. "Figuring out who in such a short amount of time will be like searching for a needle in a haystack."

"Could it be one of Patterson's security guys?" Isla asked.

"It's possible." Millie drummed her fingers on the desk. "Our best bet is to set some sort of trap, try to get a step ahead of the thief. First, we have to figure out how he or she chooses their victim."

"The bingo player was the most obvious," Isla said. "I mean, I'm sure there were hundreds of people in the theater who watched the woman win."

"True. The woman up on deck, the one whose personal belongings were stolen, was easy pickings," Millie said. "It's not uncommon for passengers to leave their stuff on the chairs all day long and never come back until late in the day."

Millie continued. "So that narrows it down to the first two thefts on deck ten. The thief wouldn't risk getting caught unless he was certain there was a reward. Both victims on deck ten claim cash was stolen. How would the culprit have known?"

There was one person who might be able to shed more light on one of the victims. "I'm going to call Cat." Millie reached for the desk phone and dialed the ship's store.

"*Ocean Treasures*. Cat Wellington speaking."

"Cat, it's Millie. I was wondering if the theft victim, the one from the lido deck, showed up to finish spending the rest of her voucher credit."

"Not yet. Today is a port day. The gift shop won't open until the ship sets sail."

"Shoot. I forgot. Please keep an eye out for her. I think the woman is one of the keys to cracking the string of thefts."

"I heard about the poor girl whose bingo winnings were taken last night." Cat tsk-tsked. "Who would take another person's lucky winnings?"

"A scumbag," Millie said. "At least Gusti is off the hook."

"I'll be covering the store floor for the rest of today. If the passenger, Valerie, returns, I'll try to pump her for information," Cat promised.

"Thanks, Cat." Millie replaced the receiver. "I don't know about you, but I'm starving. Let's go grab a bite to eat. After that, we're hosting one of my favorite events of the season."

"Christmas caroling?"

"No one wants to hear that," Millie quipped. "I can't carry a tune to save my life. It's the Christmas tree decorating. Annette is whipping up a batch of her delicious cider concoction, along with some Christmas cookies. Later this evening Nic, will be on hand for the official tree lighting ceremony."

"It sounds like fun," Isla said.

"It is, but first, it's time for lunch."

The women decided to try the ship's outdoor grill. Since it was a port day, the lines were short. Millie decided on a chilidog while Isla ordered a cheeseburger.

While they ate, Millie and Isla discussed the theft clues.

"After we finish eating, let's swing by my cabin to see if the master code works on my room safe," Isla suggested.

"That's an excellent idea."

Isla's cabin layout was identical to Millie's former cabin. The safe, located on the closet's bottom shelf, was smaller than the passenger's cabin safes, but the design and manufacturer were the same.

Millie eased onto the floor and sat Indian style while Isla fiddled with the buttons. "First, I'll lock it."

"You don't keep it locked?" Millie was shocked.

"Nope. I don't have anything of value. My paycheck is direct deposited. The only thing I have of value is an emerald ring my grandmother gave me, and I never take it off. My cabin mate uses the safe sometimes. I don't think there's anything inside right now."

Isla punched in a four-digit code. The safe made a faint whirring noise, and "locked" flashed across the screen. She gave it a gentle tug to make sure it locked.

"Now let's see if we can unlock it. What was the sequence again?"

"Press the lock button twice and then the number nine - six times," Millie said.

Isla followed Millie's instructions. The display flashed an error code.

"I'll try four times." Isla repeated the steps; pressing the number nine, four times and a second error code appeared. "It's not working."

"Try all zeroes," Millie suggested.

Isla tried again. The safe made a familiar faint whirring sound, and the door slowly opened.

It took a minute for the realization that no safe on board the Siren of the Seas was safe from the thief to sink in. "We need to let Patterson know."

Isla scrambled to her feet and gave Millie a hand up. "It could be a passenger with a security background."

"Or, it could very well be one of Patterson's men, but who?"

"The timing doesn't make sense," Isla theorized. "Think about it. Why now? Why this cruise? Ten bucks says the same person is responsible for all of the thefts. I'm not convinced it was a ship crewmember."

"We have the 'how,'" Millie said. "Now all we have to figure out is who."

The women exited the cabin, dashed down the hall to the stairs and up one deck to Patterson's office. He wasn't there, but Oscar was. "Where's Patterson?"

"He's in a meeting with Donovan and Captain Armati. They're discussing the string of thefts."

"I may have some new information about the cases." Millie corrected herself. "I mean, Isla and I discovered something interesting. Could you please ask him to call me on the radio when he's free?"

Oscar promised he would, and the women trekked upstairs to the gangway to join Andy. It was time to greet the vacationers who were returning from a day of fun in the sun.

Suharto wisely opened two of the ship's scanners to speed up the process of checking passenger's belongings. They were actually ahead of schedule with a full ten minutes before sail away.

Nic was pushing to depart early. Unfortunately, two passengers had not yet returned to the ship. It was a stressful few minutes as they waited for Suharto to radio the gate's security guard to check on their status.

Finally, the wayward passengers returned, and Suharto and his men promptly pulled the gangway. The ship began drifting away from the dock, and they were on their way.

"Now what?" Isla asked.

"It's tree trimming time," Millie said. "We haven't heard from Patterson yet. I wonder if Oscar forgot to tell him we were looking for him."

Andy perked up. "Why are you looking for Patterson?"

"We found out something very interesting about the Siren of the Seas. It's a security issue we want to bring to his attention," Millie said.

A couple approached, ending the trio's conversation.

It was time to head upstairs to the atrium where the sound of Christmas music greeted them. Several passengers offered to help with the tree decorating, and Isla began an impromptu *Rocking Around the Christmas Tree* singalong.

More passengers gathered around the upper railings to watch the tree's transformation and join in the singing.

The kitchen staff arrived and began assembling tables, filling them with containers of Annette's delicious spiced apple cider. Others arrived carrying trays of reindeer-shaped sugar cookies and other delectable sweets.

Two of the maintenance crewmembers joined them to help decorate the top of the tree. The star was the last decoration, and after it was placed on top, Millie and Isla stepped back to admire their handiwork.

Santa's red wingback chair arrived, and the workers positioned it next to the tree. The women finished the decorating by placing festively wrapped packages around the bottom.

Millie nodded her approval at the tree and decorations. "Thank you for helping me, Isla."

"It was fun. I'm glad Andy picked me to tag along with you today."

"Thank goodness, there was no sign of Tracy." Millie was more than a little relieved.

"She must've gotten off the ship while we were in port."

"Now all we have to do is get through the rest of today and tomorrow." Millie consulted her watch. "We have some time before our Christmas-themed trivia begins. I was wondering if perhaps you would like to host it."

"Could I?" Isla's eyes lit. "That would be fun."

"Absolutely." Millie was thrilled with the young woman's enthusiasm. "We'll run up there now to make sure we have all of the supplies. You'll be hosting it outside *Lucky's Casino*."

The women climbed the spiral staircase and strolled past the *Ocean Treasure's* gift shop, abruptly coming to a halt when Millie spied Cat near the front.

"Cat is waving us down." The women backtracked, making their way inside where Millie's friend met them at the door. "Valerie, the woman whose bag was stolen on the lido deck, was just in here."

"Did she spend the rest of her voucher money?"

"Yes, and she was fuming when she left."

Chapter 19

"Fuming?" Millie asked. "She was angry with you?"

"I told you her plan was to visit guest services to find out if she could cash out the remaining onboard credits," Cat said.

"No." Millie shook her head. "You never mentioned that before."

"She said she didn't need anything else and complained our logoed items were junk, which really ticked me off since I'm the one who selects the store items. You know how that goes."

"So what happened?" Millie prompted. "She was in here spending the rest of her money because guest services refused to hand over the cash?"

"Yep. She ended up buying a couple of the Tortuga rum cakes and a Siren of the Seas beach set," Cat said. "I wouldn't be surprised if she tries to return them. Wait until she finds out it's against company policy to give cash refunds."

"Is it common, I mean for people to try to return merchandise?"

"It happens all of the time."

A shopper approached carrying a cotton t-shirt. Millie waited for Cat to answer his question and the man walked away.

"She spent the rest of her money on some souvenirs, and you think she's going to try to return them?"

"She told me she wanted to cash out the credits to take to the casino. What I found most interesting is when she mentioned chatting with a fellow passenger at a poker table and discovered he was one of the theft victims."

"Cat." Millie grabbed her friend's arm. "That's it. That's the connection!"

Cat shifted her feet. "How does this link Valerie's lido deck theft to the other victims?"

"Gusti told Amit the first passenger whose cabin was broken into bragged about winning big in the casino."

"What about the others…the other passenger on deck ten?" Isla asked.

"If I can link him to the casino and maybe even the poker tables, we have a connection." Millie lowered her voice. "Think about it. Victim number one: casino player. If we can link victim number two to the casino, victim number three already told you she talked to a fellow theft victim in the casino."

"And victim number four won the bingo jackpot." Cat completed Millie's thought.

"This is it. Cat, you're a genius." Millie impulsively hugged her friend. "I've gotta go."

She exited the store, and Isla hurried to keep up. "Where are we going?"

"I met the neighbor of the second person whose cabin safe was broken into on deck ten. Her name is Amy. She's cruising with her sister, Carley." Millie abruptly stopped. "Wait a minute. We may be able to figure out if the occupants on deck ten were in the casino if they used their player's card to build up points for free comps."

"You would have to know the casino player's cabin number," Isla pointed out. "Even if they didn't use their keycard to build points, I'm pretty sure you have to sign off when you turn in your poker chips."

"I stopped by Amy's cabin the other day, to chat with her and her sister. All we have to do is head back there and locate the neighbor's cabin number. Amy and her sister are on deck ten, starboard side. I would remember the cabin if I saw it again. There's a palm tree cutout taped to the front of their cabin door."

"That should be easy."

They hustled up the stairs to deck ten and the direction of the cabin. Isla was the first to spot the palm tree. "This is it."

"When I spoke to Amy, she told me it was the cabin next door." Millie pointed to the cabin directly to the left of the palm tree'd door. "This is it. Cabin ten, six fifty-nine. Remember that."

"Ten, six fifty-nine," Isla repeated. "Now what?"

"I have a friend who works in the casino." Millie waited until they reached the end of the hall and the bank of elevators before unclipping her radio. "Brody, do you copy?"

*****

When they reached the casino, Millie motioned Brody off to the side. She briefly explained her theory that the common thread between the thefts was the casino.

"How will this help track down the thief?" Brody asked.

"I believe it's a passenger who's a regular at one of the two poker tables. Since you cover this area, I thought you might remember the regulars."

"I always remember the regulars, especially the hot-headed ones who accuse the dealers of cheating after they lose some cash. That's when I escort them out and ban them from returning."

"Have you noticed any disturbances this week at the poker tables?"

Brody gazed at Millie thoughtfully. "Nothing out of the norm. Crazy stuff goes on in here when people start losing money."

"Do you have access to the players' cards?"

"Nope. The casino workers are the only ones who have access to that information."

"But you would be able to find out if say a particular passenger in a specific cabin were to play at the poker table," Millie insisted.

"They would. I wouldn't."

Millie got right to the point. "If I gave you a cabin number, would you ask the casino workers behind the desk if the person in that cabin has been playing at the poker tables?"

"I dunno." Brody cracked his knuckles as he studied Millie. "Does Patterson know you're sticking your nose into this?"

"I'm merely asking a simple question." Millie became exasperated. "I need your help."

She sensed he was starting to cave and pressed on. "If I can tie the man in cabin ten, six fifty-nine to the poker tables, I may be able to figure out who is behind the thefts."

For a minute, Millie was certain Brody would refuse to help. Finally, he reluctantly nodded. "I'll be right back." He trudged inside the casino.

"I think he's going to find out for us," Millie told Isla excitedly.

Brody approached the counter and began speaking to one of the cashiers. He nodded a couple of times before rejoining the women near the entrance.

"Well?"

"A passenger by the name of Jason Hernandez is in cabin ten, six fifty-nine. He's a big spender and won some serious cash the first night of the cruise," Brody reported.

"At the poker table," Millie guessed.

"Yes. I remember him now. He lost a bunch of money at the table the other night. A woman came in here and gave him some grief. I asked them both to leave."

Millie's sleuthing kicked into high gear. "We have theft victim number one, who bragged to Gusti about winning big in the casino. A hundred bucks says he was playing poker. We have victim number two, whom we now know is Jason Hernandez, also a poker player."

"And a loser," Isla added.

"Correct," Millie said. "What if..." She paused as her mind raced. "What if Hernandez lied about the theft? Amy and her sister heard Hernandez and the woman who may be his wife, arguing the other night. Maybe he *claims* someone broke into his cabin, so he wouldn't have to confess to the woman he's with that he lost at the tables."

It was all beginning to make perfect sense.

"Valerie's bag was stolen up on the lido deck while she went to get some food."

"But she played in the casino and told Cat she played poker," Isla said.

"Making this connection number three to the casino and the poker tables." Millie tapped her foot on the tile floor, staring blankly into space. "Theft number four was Julia, who won a large bingo jackpot."

Brody crossed his arms, listening intently to Millie's theory. "It could be the perp. Maybe it was

Hernandez, he was feeling a little heat and switched strategies."

"Let's go with your theory. The thief followed Julia, who won the bingo jackpot, to her cabin. The person or persons waited until she and her friend left their cabin, snuck inside and stole her cash." Millie clenched her fists. "The connection is the poker tables, for at least three of the four victims. Patterson never bothered calling me back. I think it's time to pay him another visit."

Brody resumed his watch inside the casino leaving Millie and Isla to track Patterson down, which took a couple of calls on the radio. Finally, Patterson radioed back, saying he'd left the bridge and would meet them in front of *Sprinkles*, the ice cream shop.

He was already there when Millie and Isla arrived. "Has your stalker made another appearance?"

"Not yet. We haven't seen hide nor hair of Tracy. During our break, Isla and I found out some very interesting information."

Passengers strolled by, passing in close proximity to the trio.

"I think we should head outdoors where it's a little less congested," Millie suggested.

Patterson waited until they were on the open deck. "What did you find?"

"During our break, Isla and I did some online research. We not only discovered it's possible for someone with a security background or knowledge to copy a discarded keycard and turn it into a master keycard to gain access to any cabin on board this ship, but also to modify the keycard and make it virtually untraceable."

Patterson's face remained expressionless. "You say you found this on the internet?"

"Yes. We also discovered it's possible to crack the code on the ship's cabin safes." Millie briefly explained the ship's safes were given a default code at the factory. Someone with knowledge of the defaults could easily open the safes if the end user didn't take the time to reset the defaults with a new code.

"Isla and I tried it on the safe in her cabin. We entered the 'super-user mode' by pressing the lock button twice. She pressed zero six times and Voila! The safe opened."

"And you found all of this on the internet." Patterson's solemn expression deepened, and Millie suspected the ship's head of security already knew about the safe's default code and the master key.

"You know all of this, don't you?"

"I knew about the master key bypass. The average Joe wouldn't have this information. Only someone with advanced security knowledge," Patterson said. "Or someone who did exactly what you did."

"Did you know about the default setting on the safes?" Millie asked.

"I just found out, after placing a call to the head of security at corporate. As a rule, the defaults are changed before passengers set foot on the ship. It appears company policy wasn't followed." Patterson ran a hand through his hair. "As soon as the ship docks in Miami, a team of security staff from corporate will be boarding the ship and personally supervising the reset of the cabins' safes."

"That will take some time," Millie replied. "Do you know how many safes are on board?"

"Not as many as there are fleet-wide," Patterson said grimly. "I'm in the process of re-checking the backgrounds and security clearance of all of my staff, the room stewards and anyone else who may have access to passenger cabins."

"Have you figured out if there are other recent thefts on other cruise lines matching the ones we've had?" Millie asked.

255

"Yes. In fact, Exotic Voyages Cruise Line's head of security recently submitted a Cruise Line Incident Report, describing a very similar incident with the same MO. A passenger's cabin was compromised with no record of who accessed it. The passenger claims someone broke into their safe and stole a significant sum of cash."

"There was just one?" Isla, who so far remained silent, spoke.

"As far as I know. There may have been others, which weren't reported. This one was recent, and coincidentally, the ship left out of the Port of Miami. It happened last month."

Millie rubbed her palms together. "Maybe it was a test run, for the thief to figure out if he could pull it off. He or she boarded the Siren of the Seas, with a plan to ramp up the thefts."

"It may take some time to figure out who is responsible. We're comparing passenger manifests between this voyage and the Exotic Voyages ship to see if we have a passenger match. If we come up with a match, we can drill down from there."

"The culprit would be long gone," Millie pointed out.

"Unfortunately, yes."

Millie lifted both hands. "I know you don't like me butting into your investigations, but Isla and I did a little more digging around."

"Do you ever work?" Patterson joked.

"Yes." Millie scowled. "Of course I work. I do my sleuthing on my breaks."

"She does." Isla defended Millie. "We did all of our investigative work during our lunch and breaks."

"Oh no." Patterson rolled his eyes. "Not you, too?"

"We make a great team," Isla said. "Millie is one of the most exciting employees on board this ship."

"Back to your digging around," Patterson said. "You think you found something else?"

"I know I found something else," Millie said. "There's a connection between the theft victims."

Patterson looked surprised. "You found a link?"

"Yes. The connection is the casino's poker tables. I think the culprit has been scoping out his victims by targeting passengers who were winning at the poker tables or playing the poker tables." Millie explained the link between the first two theft victims and the woman who claimed items were stolen from her beach bag.

"She also played the poker tables," Millie said. "The fourth theft victim was the bingo jackpot winner. It's all about the money."

"Motive and opportunity," Patterson said.

"Yes. I think if we set up a sting, to lure the thief or thieves into striking at least one more time, there's a good chance we can literally catch them in the act."

"I see the look in your eyes. At the risk of sounding like I'm encouraging you, I'm guessing that you have an idea."

"I do. I've been giving it some thought since Isla and I connected the dots. We need two 'plants' at the poker tables tonight and tomorrow night, if necessary. It has to be someone who works on the ship behind the scenes, someone the passengers wouldn't recognize. I have an idea for at least one person who might be perfect for the job."

Chapter 20

"Annette," Patterson guessed.

"Yep. She would easily be able to pull off a sting. The only problem is…I'm not sure if she knows how to play poker," Millie said. "We would still need a second person, a plant for the second table."

Isla lifted her hand. "I've played a card game or two in the employee's lounge. I won't work because I'm all over this ship."

"True."

"My suggestion is Sharky, the card shark," Isla said.

"Sharky plays cards?" Millie wouldn't have given Sharky a second thought.

"He not only plays cards, but he's also been known to try to cheat, not that he would admit it.

He loves card games," Isla said. "It's one of the reasons he got his nickname, Sharky. That and his spiked shark-shaped hair."

"Brilliant," Millie beamed. "I wonder if he would be willing to hang out at the casino's poker tables tonight."

"It if it involves free drinks, a place to light his nasty cigars and boast about his cunning card skills, then I think it's a no-brainer," Isla said.

"This plan is starting to come together." Millie turned to Patterson. "Well? What do you think? We plant Annette and Sharky at each of the tables with a stack of poker chips. They play for some time and then cash in the chips, taking a large sum of money back to their cabin, an empty cabin, where we set a trap. The thief sneaks into the cabin and bam!" Millie smacked the palm of her hand. "We catch him or her red-handed."

"I..."

Millie could see Patterson was actually contemplating her plan, so she pushed on. "What do we have to lose? Sharky and Annette bring a pile of chips with them to the table. Win or lose, they cash in their leftover chips and take the wad of cash to an empty passenger's cabin."

"It might work," Patterson said. "It's either that or wait to see if there's a link from the passenger manifests."

"Which may or may not happen before the ship docks in Miami Saturday morning."

"You got me there."

"Our best bet is to implement the plan as soon as possible. If the culprit is going to strike again, it has to happen tonight or tomorrow," Millie said. "We could make the number of chips Annette and Sharky cash in impossible to resist."

Patterson sucked in a breath. "Despite my reservations, you've convinced me, Millie. Now, all we have to do is convince Sharky and Annette to help us out."

"You run it by Annette. Isla and I will ask Sharky," Millie said.

"It's a deal."

"We'll need two empty cabins...one for Sharky and the other for Annette. Balconies would work best. It will allow your men to hide outside."

"Bathrooms are good, too," Isla said.

"The ship is near or at capacity. We'll have to take whatever we can get," Patterson warned. "I'll get with Donovan first to secure the keycards to the rooms. He'll also be responsible for loaning us the poker chips. It's five o'clock now. Let's plan for Sharky to meet me...meet us in the galley at seven to go over the final details."

"That'll work since it's on the same deck as the casino."

The trio stepped back inside. Patterson strolled across the room to guest services while Millie and Isla headed to deck zero, where Sharky's office was located.

Millie hoped Sharky, the dayshift maintenance supervisor, was still around. His office was dark, and the door was locked. "Crud. I wonder where he is."

She reached for her radio to give him a call.

"Wait." Isla held up a hand. "Do you smell what I smell?"

Millie sniffed the air. "Yeah. It's stinky cologne."

"Sharky's stinky cologne to be exact," Isla said. "He's around here somewhere."

The women followed the smell, and it grew stronger the closer they got to the end of the long hall.

Millie heard Sharky before she saw him.

"I don't need you dopes messing around with the pallets near the gangway. We gotta leave them there so the stevedores can pull them as soon as we open the cargo door Saturday morning. We got a full ship next week, and we can't afford to have another backup like we did last week."

They rounded the corner, and Millie found Sharky comfortably seated on his decked out scooter, an unlit cigar dangling from his mouth.

"Sharky Kiveski, aka the card shark. Just the man we're looking for."

"Millie." Sharky straightened. "I was thinkin' about you the other day, right after I unloaded a crate full of Christmas reindeer with Andy's name on 'em."

"I found a home for them, although Andy told me there are more waiting on the dock," Millie said.

"Thanks for the warning. I'll have my guys take them straight upstairs and drop them in Andy's office."

"That's not why I'm..." She motioned to Isla. "Why we're here. We need your help."

Sharky pulled the cigar from his mouth. "Another favor?"

"Sort of. Actually, the favor is for Dave Patterson."

"I didn't do it." Sharky motioned with his hands. "I've been stuck here on this deck for four days straight and haven't even had time to visit the employee lounge, right Isla?"

"Not that we missed you," Isla muttered.

"What's that supposed to mean?" Sharky shot her an angry glare.

"Patterson needs you to help with a sting operation up in the casino this evening and possibly tomorrow night."

"The casino?" Sharky perked up. "What kind of sting operation?"

"Isla told us you like to play poker."

"They don't call me Ace for nothing," Sharky boasted.

"They don't call you Ace. They call you Sharky because you're a card shark," Isla snorted.

Millie took a step closer. "Patterson is going to give you a pile of poker chips to take to the poker table. You need to play conservatively and hang onto most of them."

"What if I win? I mean...what if Patterson loans me a bunch of poker chips and I win?"

Millie could see Sharky was warming to the plan. "You'll need to take it up with Patterson what happens if you win. Back to the sting. We need you to make the poker chips last, play well into the evening, striking up a conversation with the other players about how you plan to cash in the winnings and walk off the ship with a boatload of money."

Sharky interrupted. "Is the sting because of a cheater, because I can spot someone cheating at cards a mile away."

Isla started to say something. Millie gave her a quick look, and she promptly closed her mouth.

"We believe a passenger on board the ship is targeting other passengers who are winning large sums of money in the casino. They're waiting for them to exit the casino and then following them back to their cabin."

Millie explained her theory the thief waited for the passenger to exit their cabin. "After the passenger leaves, the thief sneaks inside, breaks into the cabin safe and steals their winnings."

"So you need me to play for a while..."

"Conservatively," Millie reminded him.

"Conservatively," Sharky repeated. "Later in the evening, I cash in the chips, make a big deal of returning to my cabin, stick the loot in the safe, walk out and wait for someone to break in and steal it."

"In a nutshell. Patterson is working out the details as far as the exact amount of chips and the cabin you'll be using for the sting."

"I've been by the casino. There are two poker tables."

"Annette is the other plant, and she'll be playing at the other table."

"Can you put us in the same cabin together?" Sharky asked.

"Oh brother," Millie groaned. "No. For two reasons. Number one, Annette would never agree and number two, you need to pretend you don't know each other."

"Bummer. Well, it was worth a try." Sharky waved dismissively. "I'll do it on one condition."

"Does it involve food?"

"No, but that's an excellent idea. I want to smoke my cigars while I'm playing. It helps me concentrate."

"I see no problem with bringing your cigars. Smoking is allowed in the casino," Millie said.

"Good. Cuz if I can't smoke my old Swisher Sweets, then I ain't gonna play."

"We'll see you up in the galley at seven sharp." Millie gave Sharky a mock salute, and she and Isla retraced their steps.

"That went well," Isla said.

"Considering we're dealing with Sharky, I have to agree."

"Do you think your plan will work?"

"I hope so. We're running out of time. Besides, what have we got to lose?"

"This is so exciting. Now, all we have to do is finish our shift and meet the others in the galley."

"And pray the sting doesn't blow up in our faces."

Chapter 21

Millie and Isla were the first to arrive. They found Annette in the galley, the expression on her face a perfect mirror of the *Born to be Wild* rocker t-shirt she wore.

"I love your t-shirt," Isla said.

"It was a gift from my neighbor before I joined the Siren of the Seas years ago. I thought I threw it away." Annette glanced behind Millie. "Where's the plague?"

"If you're referring to Sharky, I'm sure he's on his way."

"Packing Swisher Sweets, no doubt," Isla joked.

"Great. He's going to stink the place up with those disgusting tubes of grossness?"

"It was part of the deal," Millie mumbled. "At least I didn't agree to his request to put the two of you in the same cabin."

"What?" Annette roared.

Before Millie could elaborate, Patterson strolled into the galley, accompanied by Oscar and another of the assistant security guards.

Sharky brought up the rear. "This is a farce," he whined.

Patterson ignored Sharky and kept walking. "You look...wild, Annette."

"I've been called worse. The shirt fit the mood. Let's leave it at that. You got the goods?"

"Yep." Patterson reached into his pocket, pulled out a clear plastic bag filled with poker chips and set them on the counter. "You sure you're up for this?"

"I haven't played poker in a few years. Even if I lose, that's not the point," Annette said.

"Correct. The only thing you need to do is make the chips last and walk away from the table with a large pile."

Millie picked up a red chip. "This is a five-dollar chip."

"The green are twenty-five, and the black represents a hundred," Annette rattled off.

"Which means hang onto as many black chips as possible." Patterson wagged his finger at Sharky. "Got that? You can play. You can even keep any winnings over the amount of chips I gave you."

Patterson outlined the plan...Annette and Sharky would each make their way to one of the poker tables, playing for several hours and striking up conversations with the other players. They would then make a point of leaving the table with at least a couple thousand in chips.

"Take the remaining chips to the cashier; cash them out and then slowly." Patterson stressed *slowly*. "Walk out of the casino."

He pointed to Annette. "Annette, you're in balcony cabin ten two sixty-seven. Here's the cabin keycard."

Patterson handed her a keycard, and she slipped it into her jeans pocket.

He turned to Sharky. "You're in cabin four fifty-two, an ocean view cabin. While you play, we'll have two of our security guys hiding out in each of the cabins, inside the cabin's bathroom. After cashing in the chips, take the money to the cabin, place it in the safe, using a code of four sevens. Lock the safe, exit the cabin and return here."

"Any questions?" Patterson shot Sharky a pointed stare.

"I got it," Sharky mumbled. "We'll both play for a few hours, take the chips to the cashier, cash them in, take the cash to the cabin, lock it in the safe using four sevens for the code and then come back here. You want to wrap this operation up by eleven, so we leave the casino sometime between ten and eleven."

"Precisely. Annette, you head out first. Go through the galley, into the dining room and then circle around to the casino."

Annette gathered up the chips, slipped them into her sling purse and exited the galley.

Patterson waited a good ten minutes before signaling for Sharky to follow behind. He waited until Sharky was gone.

"Brody is keeping an eye on both of them. I have another security guard in street clothes stationed outside the casino. My other guys will take their place inside the cabins shortly. What could go wrong?"

Millie sucked in a breath. "Hopefully, nothing. On the other hand, maybe everything."

*****

The hours dragged as Millie and Isla made their rounds. They went top to bottom, forward to aft, checking on the various evening activities.

Isla hosted another round of trivia, followed by co-hosting a round of karaoke.

At each event, Millie searched the crowds for Tracy. Once, during the karaoke, she thought she caught a glimpse of her standing near the door. When she looked again, the woman was gone.

Karaoke ended, and the women headed upstairs for the *Moonlight Madness* festivities on the lido deck. It was also Mexican fiesta night.

There were piñatas, face painting for the kids, a tortilla eating competition, topped off by a sombrero ring toss.

The women managed to grab a quick bite to eat before helping the singers and dancers backstage during the headliner show.

At ten-thirty, Millie couldn't stand it any longer, and Isla and she headed to the galley to see if Annette or Sharky had returned.

Annette was inside, chatting with Oscar.

"You're back."

"Yep. I just got here. I even managed to make a coupla bucks at the poker table. Patterson told me I could keep it." Annette pulled a wad of bills from her purse.

Millie chuckled. "It looks like the sting was worth your while. You dropped the cash in the safe and took off?"

"Of course. I left the cash and a little something else behind." Annette pulled her iPad from one of the cabinets, flipped the top and turned it on.

"You hid a spy cam in the cabin?"

"Why not? Patterson never said I couldn't. His guys watched me do it and didn't stop me."

"What if the culprit goes after Sharky and not you?"

"I snuck Sharky a spy cam, too, during a bathroom break. We can watch both cabins on a split screen." Annette began fiddling with the mouse. "It'll only take a minute to get these up and running."

"I don't know." Oscar cleared his throat. "Patterson might not like this."

Annette shot him a quick glance. "Do you want me to go back and get it?"

Oscar shook his head "no."

A split screen appeared. One of the cameras came in clearly. The other was grainy. "We don't have a visual on Sharky's camera yet. He should be setting it up any time now."

There were some flashes of light on the second screen and then it came into view. Sharky's fin of hair appeared followed by his face, which filled the screen.

He blew a kiss at the camera and then after a few more dizzying seconds, the image became clear.

"Disgusting," Annette grunted.

"At least he planted it," Millie said.

Oscar, Annette, Millie and Isla focused their attention on the screen until the sound of the galley door opening caught Millie's attention.

Sharky strolled in. "Did you get my kiss?"

"Yeah. It made me want to throw up," Annette said. "I wish the screens were bigger. I left my reading glasses downstairs."

"You can borrow mine," Millie said. "I can see the screen." She handed Annette her reading glasses.

They all crowded around the small screen and silently watched.

Millie shifted uncomfortably. She straightened as she stretched. "I'm sure Patterson is hanging out near one of the cabins and has someone else keeping an eye on the other one."

"Felippe," Oscar said.

"Not you?" Millie lifted a brow.

"Not this time. He wanted me to stay here with you."

Millie laughed. "So you could keep an eye on us and make sure we didn't mess up his sting."

Oscar's face turned red. "Something like that."

"I see movement in my cabin." Annette lifted the iPad, giving them all a clear view of the entrance to the cabin.

They squeezed in closer, and Millie sucked in a breath as she watched the door close. A dark figure appeared, followed by a burst of light.

Millie stared at the screen. "What happened?"

Annette rubbed her brow. "My guess is they got spooked and took off."

"Great." Millie sucked in a breath. "The perp got away."

"The show is over, folks." Annette reached for the iPad.

"Wait." A bright light shot across the screen. "I think they changed their mind," Millie said.

The dark figure crossed in front of the screen again before slowly turning to face the hidden surveillance camera.

The culprit's shadowy features appeared; clear enough for Millie to recognize the intruder. "Will you look at that?"

"Who is it?" Annette asked.

"It's Valerie Yost," Oscar said. "She is the woman who reported items stolen from her beach bag."

The woman flung the closet door open, partially obstructing their view. Millie guessed she was attempting to access the contents of the safe.

Valerie reappeared and held up a stash of cash. "She has the money. I hope Patterson is on it," Annette said.

A shadow suddenly blocked the screen. The shadow disappeared, followed by a burst of bright light and then nothing.

"Someone just rushed her. It's a takedown," Annette said.

Millie waited for something else to happen, but the screen remained black, with only intermittent bursts of light.

"We missed the good stuff," Isla said. "Too bad there wasn't any sound."

"But they got her." Millie stared at the screen in disbelief. "Cat. Cat said Valerie mentioned wanting to cash in her remaining credits to use in the casino. It all makes perfect sense."

Millie continued. "So she hit the poker tables with a plan to steal from some of the other poker players. When she ran out of money and ran into trouble finding victim number three, she hatched a plan to pretend she was also a victim, hoping she could cash in on her alleged loss. All this time I thought it was Jason Hernandez."

"It wouldn't appear suspicious to security. Yost already knew about the other two legitimate thefts since she was the one who committed them," Annette said. "It was almost the perfect crime."

"I bet when Patterson matches our passenger manifest to the manifest of the other cruise ship, that reported a similar theft, they'll find Valerie Yost's name."

It was another hour before Patterson and his men returned to the galley. "The sting was a success."

"You nabbed, Valerie Yost, aka the lido deck victim. She reported a theft, hoping to throw off your investigation," Millie said.

"How do you know?" Patterson's eyes narrowed.

"Surveillance cameras." Oscar pointed to Annette's iPad. "We watched the takedown."

Patterson cast his eyes skyward. "Why am I surprised?"

"We merely watched from the sidelines," Annette said. "So what's the scoop?"

"Millie nailed it. Valerie Yost is a thief and a scammer, not to mention a heavy gambler. Before I came here, I stopped by my office and left a message for the other ship's security officer to see if Valerie Yost was also a passenger on their ship."

"Where is she now?" Isla asked.

"She's in the holding cell and none too happy about it. Ms. Yost is threatening to sue us."

"Like we haven't heard that before," Oscar said.

"The show's over," Patterson said. "Thank you, Sharky and Annette, for helping with the sting."

"I even made a little extra cash." Annette turned to Sharky. "How did you do?"

"Eh. I had fun playing poker, got to smoke my Swisher Sweets and sit close to my babe." Sharky made googly eyes at Annette, and she punched him in the arm. "Wipe that look off your face."

"Annette." Sharky appeared genuinely hurt. "We could be so good together."

"Over my dead body." Annette shooed Sharky out of the galley.

Patterson, Oscar and the other security guards followed behind. "I need to head back to the office. I have a ton of paperwork to fill out."

Isla, Annette and Millie were the last to leave.

"Thanks for taking one for the team," Millie said.

"You're welcome. It was like old times," Annette said. "I would never admit it to Sharky, but it was fun. I was watching him. He's a pretty good poker player, although not as good as me."

"Because he cheats," Isla said.

"It doesn't surprise me." Annette covered her mouth to stifle her yawn. "The takedown wore me out. I've gotta be back up here tomorrow morning at six. I think it's time to call it a night."

The trio paused when they reached the stairwell.

"I'll be glad when tomorrow is over," Millie said.

"Not me." Isla shook her head. "I had so much fun tonight. I hope tomorrow is just as exciting."

"The highlight of my week will be Saturday morning when we dock in Miami," Millie said. "I'm glad Valerie was caught."

She told her friends goodnight and waited until they disappeared around the corner before reaching into her pocket for her keycard.

Millie caught a sudden movement out of the corner of her eye right before she felt a searing pain in the back of her neck.

Chapter 22

Millie stumbled forward and then fell to the floor, landing on her hands and knees.

She shifted back, just in time to see Annette leap through the air and knock Millie's assailant, Tracy Robinson, to the floor.

The women wrestled back and forth, as a helpless Millie tried desperately to find an opening to help her friend.

But Annette didn't need any help. She quickly subdued Tracy, pinning her to the ground. "Call Patterson," she grunted breathlessly.

Millie jerked her radio off her belt. "Charlie. Charlie. Charlie on deck seven forward!" She yelled.

Tracy twisted back and forth in a desperate attempt to escape Annette's ironclad grip, but it was no use. The woman was no match for Annette.

The clatter of thundering boots filled the corridor, and several security guards burst on the scene, surrounding the trio.

"This passenger attacked me." Millie pointed to Tracy, who let loose a string of cuss words.

The security guards quickly took control of the situation, restraining the struggling woman and finally escorting her from the area.

Oscar hung back. "Millie Armati. Haven't you had enough excitement for tonight?"

"You would think so." Millie gingerly touched the tender spot on the back of her head and noticed a small amount of blood. "What happened?"

"She came after you with a steak knife." Annette pointed to one of the ship's steak knives, nearby.

Oscar motioned Millie to lean forward and examined the wound on her neck. "It looks like she nicked you. You may want to have Doctor Gundervan take a look at it."

"I will." Millie turned to Annette. "What made you come back here?"

"I remembered I had your reading glasses and figured you might need them tomorrow." Annette handed Millie her glasses. "I rounded the corner in time to see Tracy sneak up behind you."

"I owe you one. No, I owe you more than one."

"It was nothing." Annette waved dismissively. "Looks like I still got it."

"You got something all right." Oscar picked up the knife, turning it over in his hand. "Remind me never to mess with you."

"I only go after the bad guys," Annette joked.

Oscar jotted down a few notes. After he finished, Millie and Annette promised they would stop by the security office in the morning to finish the report.

They waited for Oscar to leave and Millie turned to her friend. "I'm sure you're really whupped now."

"I think I got my second wind. I'll see you in the morning?"

"Sure." Millie waited for Annette to leave, but she stayed put. "Is there something else?"

"I figured I would hang out for a minute to make sure you make it home safely."

"Of course." Millie impulsively hugged her friend and climbed the stairs to the bridge.

Annette trailed behind.

"I don't know what I ever did to deserve a friend like you, but whatever it was, I'm glad I did." Millie slid her keycard into the door and slipped onto the bridge.

Nic was standing in front of the control panels. He did a double take when he saw his wife. "I was beginning to wonder when you were coming home. How was your day?"

"It was a pain in the neck, literally." Millie limped toward her husband. "Where do I begin?"

*****

The next morning, Millie's only reminder of Tracy's attack was the gauze bandage Gundervan had applied, along with a slight sting on the back of her neck.

She woke early, anxious to track Patterson down to get an update on Valerie Yost's detainment.

Annette was already in Patterson's office when Millie arrived.

"Millie Armati." Patterson shook his head. "I can barely keep up with you. How is your wound?"

"Fine." Millie touched the bandage. "Doctor Gundervan said it's a small nick and I'll be fine. What happened to Tracy Robinson?"

"She's under cabin arrest and will remain there until the ship docks tomorrow. She'll have a police escort to the local police station."

"And Valerie Yost?" Millie inquired.

"You don't miss a beat, do you?" Patterson asked.

"Not if I can help it," Millie shot back.

"Yost's name is on Exotic Voyages Cruise line's manifest from the cruise in question, where a similar theft took place. Having caught her in the act of stealing the planted money from the safe, not to mention Annette's surveillance footage of her theft, we have a solid case to press charges. She will also have a police escort off the ship."

He continued. "We haven't dug into her background yet. I wouldn't be surprised if she worked for a security company or has some sort of security background."

"I still have one question, something that has been bothering me since last night." Millie perched on the edge of her chair. "Why were the cabin doors in the first two thefts left ajar?"

"I think I can answer that," Annette said. "Yost wanted it to look like the cabin steward was either careless or responsible, hoping security would focus on the ship's employees."

"Instead of other passengers," Millie mused. "It looks like I have another solved mystery under my belt. I'm ten for zero."

"Not yet," Patterson disagreed. "Donovan and I met with Andy this morning. He said something about missing reindeer and asked if he could check the surveillance cameras to see if he can figure out who is stealing them."

"Are you going to let him?"

"No." Patterson started laughing. "I told him he needed to put you on the case and he agreed. We're going to call it the *Reindeer and Robberies* investigation."

The end.

If you enjoyed reading "Reindeer & Robberies," please take a moment to leave a review. It would be greatly appreciated. Thank you.

The series continues...Book 16 in the "Cruise Ship Cozy Mysteries" series coming soon!

Get Free eBooks and More

Sign up for my Free Cozy Mysteries Newsletter to get free and discounted ebooks, giveaways & new releases!

hopecallaghan.com/newsletter

Meet the Author

Hope loves to connect with her readers! Connect with her today!

Never miss another book deal! Text the word Books to 33222

Visit **hopecallaghan.com/newsletter** for special offers, free books, and soon-to-be-released books!

Pinterest:
https://www.pinterest.com/cozymysteriesauthor/

Facebook:
https://www.facebook.com/authorhopecallaghan/

Instagram:
https://www.instagram.com/hopecallaghanauthor/

Hope Callaghan is an American author who loves to write Christian books, especially Christian Mystery and Cozy Mystery books. She has written more than 50 mystery books (and counting) in five series.

In March 2017, Hope won a Mom's Choice Award for her book, "Key to Savannah," Book 1 in the Made in Savannah Cozy Mystery Series.

Born and raised in a small town in West Michigan, she now lives in Florida with her husband.

She is the proud mother of one daughter and a stepdaughter and stepson. When she's not doing the thing she loves best - writing books - she enjoys cooking, traveling and reading books.

Spiced Apple Cider Recipe

From the Kitchen of Renate Pennington

Ingredients:

4 cups apple cider

½ - ¾ cup orange juice

½ cup water

Spices: 2 cinnamon sticks

½ tsp. all spice

½ tsp. whole cloves

Directions:

-Mix all ingredients except for the all spice and cloves.

- Place all spice and cloves in a tea strainer.

-Add tea strainer containing spices to pot.

-Simmer in 2-quart pot for at least 30 minutes.

Amit's Reindeer Cheese Ball Recipe

Ingredients:

12 oz. – cream cheese, softened
¼ cup bacon bits
¼ cup smoked ham, diced
1/3 cup scallion, chopped
1 tbsp. green olives, chopped
1 tsp. Worcestershire sauce
1 cup chopped walnuts

Directions:

-Mix the cream cheese, bacon bits, smoked ham, scallion, olives and Worcestershire sauce.
-Form mixture into a ball.
-Cover and refrigerate until firm, at least 2 hours.
-Place a large sheet of waxed or parchment paper on a flat surface.
-Sprinkle walnuts on top of the paper.
-Roll the firm cheese ball in the walnuts until completely covered.

-Transfer the cheese ball to a serving plate or rewrap with waxed paper.
-Refrigerate until needed. *

*We left the cheese ball in the fridge overnight and it tasted even better the next day.

*I substituted tortilla chips for the antlers, added pimento stuffed green olives for the eyes and a slice of pepperoni for the nose.

Printed in Great Britain
by Amazon